Like the others.

That's what Marian had said to him on the phone.

Licia has killed herself.

Killed herself.

Her self.

Like the others.

Yes, those were the words.

The others.

A mist came over his eyes and he hit the steering wheel with his fist again and again.

"Alicia," he whispered. "Why did you do what they did? Why . . . ?"

The Dark Corridor

Jay Bennett

FAWCETT JUNIPER • NEW YORK

RLI: $\dfrac{\text{VL 4 \& up}}{\text{IL 7 \& up}}$

A Fawcett Juniper Book
Published by Ballantine Books
Copyright © 1988 by Jay Bennett

Library of Congress Catalog Card Number: 88-20692

ISBN 0-449-70337-1

This edition published by arrangement with Franklin Watts, Inc.

Manufactured in the United States of America

First Ballantine Books Edition: October 1990

For Cathleen
Ever dear to me

Chapter

1

He was listening to the Brahms Violin Concerto, the last movement, he remembered it was the last movement, close to the shimmering end, when the phone rang.

Sunlight was coming through the high clear windows and down over the rug, streaming over the white rug, making it look pure and untouched.

It was a brilliant morning sun, brilliant and strangely soothing.

He kept looking at the glowing rug and thinking to himself, this is the last day of summer. The last day of the long, lonely summer.

Soon Autumn will come, cold and bleak. And its savage rains will wash away the memories of the three deaths.

Then he will be able to sleep again.

The phone still rang, coldly and insistently.

He picked it up reluctantly.

"Hello."

He didn't turn off the music.

"Kerry?"

"Yes?"

"Kerry, can you hear me?"

It was Alicia's mother.

No.

It was Alicia's stepmother. Her real mother had split, vanished. Like smoke. Years ago. Nobody ever thought of her anymore.

This was the stepmother talking to him.

"What is it, Marian?"

He had to ask her again.

"Kerry, something terrible has happened."

He heard her voice quiver and break and he waited.

"Alicia has killed herself."

She said it again.

"Licia has killed herself."

And again.

"Herself."

Like a dark litany in a monotonous flat tone.

"What?" he said in disbelief.

"Like the others. Just like the others."

And then, just before he could speak again, the phone went dead.

He slowly put the receiver back onto its hook.

A soft click.

Within that swirling heart of the music he could hear the soft final click and he knew that his life had started its slow walk down the long dark corridor.

Life is a dark corridor that leads to a dusty death, Kerry.

No, Alicia.

It is. It is, dear Kerry. You will find out. Soon enough.

He sat by the silent phone for what seemed like a long time but was only a few seconds. Then he got up and went quietly out to the sunswept house, leaving the front door fully open and the music still playing. The sound drifted through the open door with shimmering, life-beckoning beauty.

He stopped once on the broad patio, just before descending the red brick steps, and looked back into the now empty house, back to the glistening white rug, and he thought of his father away in Europe with his new bride. His father had bought the rug for her as a house present, that's what he told Kerry with a vacant, almost indifferent look in his pale blue eyes.

That's what she wanted, Kerry. A new rug. Just that.

I see.

You've got to keep them happy, his father said.

Sure.

Give them what they want. Remember that, his father continued.

I will.

Within reason, of course.

Of course, Kerry said.

Keep them happy and you'll be happy.

I'll be sure to remember that, Dad. Very sure.

You're putting me on.

No. Not at all, Kerry said.

The pale blue eyes had become cool and studying.

Putting me on. I wish you wouldn't try that on me, his father said.

I won't, Dad.

He thought of his father away for the whole summer, leaving him alone in the house. Sending postcards. An occasional call to see if the house hadn't burnt down.

So what? he thought dully.

That's the way we both wanted it.

We're just two shadows living with each other.

And now he's bringing in another shadow.

Then Kerry turned away from the blinding sight of the

white rug and went to his car and as he walked he whispered once.

"Alicia."

That was all he said.

He started the motor of his sun-warmed car, and only then did he realize that he was cold, icily cold. So cold that his hands trembled. They slipped off the steering wheel, the palms moist.

But his eyes were dry.

No tears.

No tears at all.

They would come later.

Chapter

2

As he drove along the waterfront road, the one that ran alongside the Sound, he kept looking out at the boats and thinking of Alicia, thinking of the first time he had ever seen her. He had come down to the dock and was just sitting there, looking out over the water when he heard a soft, easy voice close to him.

"You have a nice profile."

He turned and there she was looking down at him, the sun flowing over her dark, long hair.

He didn't speak.

"Now I can see that you have blue eyes. Gentle blue eyes."

He was still silent.

"You're new here," she said.

"Uh-huh."

"The house on Chestnut Lane?" she asked.

"How did you know?" he said.

She smiled. "This is a small town. You know everything in a small town. Especially when most everybody has money and status. It's like coming into a club. An exclusive club."

"Oh."

"You're Kerry Lanson and your father is a television executive. A network wheel."

"He's a wheel."

"I'm Alicia Kent. My father is Peter Kent. You know of him, I'm sure."

Kerry shook his head. "No."

She laughed softly and he liked the sound of her low voice and the gentle play of light on her lips when she spoke.

"You will," she said. "He's an awfully wealthy man and a powerful one. I'm his only daughter. No sons."

"Oh."

"Someday I'll have an awful lot of money, all my own, to throw away as I please. Just as I please."

"That's good," he said quietly.

"You don't like that, do you?"

A slight breeze had come up. He glanced from her to the stretch of rippling blue water.

"I didn't say that," he said.

"But it's there. You don't like the very rich, do you?"

He turned away from the scattered white sails and back to her.

"I didn't say that either."

"You didn't."

They looked directly at each other and he saw for an instant, only an instant, a wistful, lonely look flash into the deep brown eyes and then vanish.

"You didn't," she said again.

Her fingers played with a diamond ring that was on one of her long, tapering fingers, played unconsciously, turning it round and round. The facets of the diamond glittered in the sunlight.

"I don't like the very rich either," she said in a low

6

voice. "When they throw away money, only on themselves. Only themselves."

Then she laughed again.

"So you see I'll end up not liking myself," Alicia said.

"That's the worst thing a person can do," he said.

"The worst?"

"Yes. You've got nowhere to go when you let that happen to you. You're up against a blank wall. A dark one. It's a real scary scene."

"Scary?"

"Yes."

She smiled wistfully at him.

"I guess you're right. It can get scary."

He looked directly up at her, his eyes quietly studying her.

She was almost as tall as he was and she had a quiet, lithe beauty. She moved with an easy grace. Easy and sure of herself.

Alicia.

Alicia.

"Do you like it here, Kerry?"

"Like it?" he asked.

"Yes?"

She sat down on an overturned rowboat and talked to him as though she had known him all of her short life.

He remembered that so distinctly.

She wore cheap old jeans, scuffed white sneakers, old, and a new white shirt which had a designer's insignia stitched over the breast pocket.

The shirt gleamed pure and untouched in the sun.

He remembered that.

The white, white shirt.

"Do you, Kerry?" she asked again.

He thought a while before answering.

"Can't say yet," he said.

7

"Do you think you will?"

And his answer seemed important to her.

"Maybe."

"And maybe you won't?"

"It could turn out that way."

Her eyes darkened.

"Life is a senseless gamble," she said in a low and almost bitter voice. "Isn't it? We never know how it's going to turn out, do we?"

"Senseless? A gamble?"

"Yes."

He shook his head. "I didn't say that."

She smiled gently at him. "You didn't. I did."

They sat silent and watched a passing boat, a white figure on the desk waved and called out her name and she waved back.

And while she was waving, without turning to Kerry, she spoke.

"You father had three marriages."

"Two."

She turned back to him and smiled. "He'll have another one. They always do. Which one are you from?"

"The first."

"A love child," she said.   .

He grinned. "You can call it that."

"Your mother dead?" she asked.

He shook his head. "She's out on the coast. Does a news show."

"Oh."

"How come you didn't know that?" he asked.

"Some things I don't know."

"Uh-huh."

He reached down and picked up a sun-dried stick and threw it over the water, watched it spin lazily and then drift away.

"And your father?" he asked.

She held up two long and tapering fingers.

Patrician, he thought. And he said to himself. Yes. Yes, there is something definitely patrician about you. As though you were born to rule.

To have your way always. And always.

And you know it.

Yet something deep inside of you doesn't like the whole deal. Completely rejects it. And you don't know what to do about it.

He heard her speak to him.

"Only two marriages," she said.

"That all?" he asked.

She nodded. "That's all. My mother split. Got up one morning, sat down in her brand new Jaguar and rode off into the sunset. Without saying goodbye."

"Not even to you?" he asked.

She didn't answer.

She gave the ring a few glittering turns before she spoke again.

"And now I have a stepmother. She has a daughter named Laurie and we all get along. So what's new, Kerry, since I last saw you?"

"Nothing, Alicia," he said gently.

He wanted to reach out and touch her hand but he didn't.

"Are you going to college?" she asked.

"Yes."

"What are you going to major in?"

"I don't know yet. How about you?"

A roguish smile came into her brown eyes.

"I'm a whiz when I feel like being one. Peter Kent wants me to take over the Kent empire one day in the not so distant future. I'll wait and see."

He looked at her and slowly studied her.

"So you are a brain?" he said.

She laughed. "A genius percentile. All the test scores are agreed."

"You're putting me on," he said.

She shook her head and smiled. "Telling it to you as it is."

"Are you?"

"Yes," she said. "I'm terrific in economics, art, science and what have you. Higher mathematics is like arithmetic to me. It's all a breeze."

"All a breeze," he said wryly.

She put her hand out and touched him softly on the bare arm. He quivered and didn't know why.

"Kerry, I've been that way since I was a child. I'm eighteen now."

"I don't believe you," he said.

"That I'm eighteen? I'm the same age as you are. Just three days older."

He stared at her. "What?"

"You were born December 24th. You're a Christmas Eve baby," she said.

"How did you know that?"

"I find out things when I want to."

"And you wanted to."

"Yes."

He looked at her and then he said quietly, "I believe you."

"That I'm your age or that I'm a genius?"

"Both."

She laughed.

"Why? What made you change your mind so quickly?"

He didn't know why. But he spoke anyway. "I guess 'it was the color of her eyes,' as they say in songs."

"My eyes?"

"Yes."

There was a slight flush on her face. "Now you're putting me on," she said.

He grinned. "Isn't that the way of the world these days?"

"To put each other on?" she asked.

"Yes."

"To deceive each other?"

"All the time," he said.

"You're becoming cynical."

"Am I?"

"And it's not like you at all, Kerry."

"How do you know what I'm like? You just met me."

"I know," Alicia said.

"Oh. I forgot. You have ways of finding things out."

"Yes."

Then they both looked at each other and began to laugh.

And he knew that he cared for her.

A lot.

Yet deep underneath it all he felt a strange fear beginning to stir within him. A fear that a shadow had fallen over his life. And would never leave it again.

Never.

Chapter

3

He remembered getting out of bed that first night, the night after their first meeting, and going to his window and looking out at the dark, moonless sky and thinking of her.

The diamond glittering on her long tapering finger.

Thinking of her. Ever thinking of her.

The oval patrician face with the dark profound eyes.

The way she held her head when she spoke to him.

The way she let her voice lower to a whisper and then fade into the sunlight.

The way she. . . .

And a line of an old, old poem came tolling softly into his mind, tolling again and again.

You were born for death.

Born for death.

Death.

"You were born for death, Alicia," he murmured.

And as he heard the whispered words fade into the motionless night, a chill went through him and his hands trembled.

He kept staring through the window at the black sky a long time. A very long time.

Then as he lay on his white bed and looked up at the dark ceiling he asked himself over and over again: Why did I think that of her? Why did I say it? Where did it come from?

He finally fell asleep still asking the question.

There was no answer.

When he awoke with the sunlight filling his room, he had forgotten the question and the black night.

All that remained was the sunlight.

Chapter

4

He was swimming with her in the pool when Marian came out to them, the sun glistening on her straight blonde hair and tanned arms and legs.

"Licia," she said.

Alicia stopped swimming and turned to her stepmother. "Yes?"

"Your father wants to speak to you."

Alicia waved her hand.

"Oh. Tell him I'll call him back."

Marian shook her head gently. "It's from San Francisco."

"Tell him, Marian," Alicia said.

"Please, Licia. He says it's important."

Alicia splashed a handful of sparkling water onto Kerry. "He always says it's important. What isn't in his frenetic world?"

"Please, Licia. Just this once," her stepmother said. There was a bit of a flush on Marian's cheeks, but her voice was calm and patient.

14

"Did you tell him I have a guest?" Alicia asked.

"Yes. And he apologized and sent his regards to Kerry."

"He likes Kerry."

"Yes. He likes Kerry," Marian said.

"And admires him."

"He does."

"And he's happy when I'm with Kerry," Alicia said.

"Alicia," her stepmother said.

"Good. I'll call him back this afternoon. I'm sure it can wait."

"It can't."

Alicia swam back to the edge of the pool and looked up with a smile at her stepmother. "How do you know that?"

"Because he said it can't," Marian said calmly.

"Did he?"

"He emphasized it. Knowing what you were going to say, Licia."

Alicia looked almost desperately to Kerry and shook her head.

"Oh, all right," she said.

He watched her slowly get out of the pool, the water dripping over her tall, lithe body, and then he saw her go to a brightly colored towel and leisurely dry herself while Marian stood waiting.

Marian was much shorter than Alicia and had a strong, athletic figure. Peter Kent had met her on a golf course while she was playing in a minor tournament. Her face was a pleasant one, smooth and plain.

Kerry thought her to be in her mid-forties.

He liked her. And he felt that she liked him.

"Licia, he's in conference," Marian said.

Alicia tossed her head.

"He's always in conference. He's a tycoon. They're always in conference. Doing what? Meeting with other tycoons. How could it be otherwise?" She laughed, a low

15

almost harsh laugh. "Someone ought to write a musical and call it Conference of the Tycoons. Kerry, can you write music? Of course you can. I'll do the book. Marian, we'll get Peter Kent to put up the money. Five million should do it. A half million to buy off the critics and we'll have a smash hit."

"Licia," Marian said again.

Alicia finished drying her hair and then picked up a robe and put it on.

"I'll only be a few minutes, Kerry."

"No sweat. Take your time," he said.

She waved to him and he watched her go into the house and disappear into the long shadows.

The last thing he saw was a gleam of light on her hair and then that vanished and only the shadows remained.

Marian sighed and then sat down on one of the pool chairs and lit a cigarette.

She looked down at Kerry and smiled.

"She's a queen, isn't she? Royalty." She said it in a gentle but exasperated voice.

"Uh-huh," Kerry agreed.

"She always gives him a hard time."

"What does he want with her?" he asked.

"To ask her advice on some important project. I'm sure it's that," Marian said.

"What?" He stared up at her.

"Yes, Kerry." Marian smiled and nodded. "Licia's been giving him advice off and on ever since she was sixteen."

"To Peter Kent?" he asked.

"To him."

"Unbelievable," Kerry said.

"Isn't it?" she said. Marian smoked and looked over his head into the sun-filled sky and then she turned back to him. "Lately, he's been coming to her more often."

"And Alicia?" he asked.

16

"Depends on her moods."

"Alicia has her moods," Kerry said.

Marian smiled and nodded. "She does."

A silvery plane passed overhead, its wings gleaming.

Neither of them spoke.

For some reason, Kerry thought again of the glittering facets of Alicia's diamond.

And then the glittering plane was gone.

Marian looked away from the sky and back to Kerry.

It was then that she said something that Kerry never forgot.

"Licia can be the most wonderful creature in the universe. Kind and generous and just good to be with."

She can, Kerry thought.

"A real joy," Marian continued. "She's made my life very pleasant here. I'm sure she cares for my daughter Laurie and me. Very much. I'm sure of that."

Marian paused and he saw her blue, calm eyes go cold.

"But she can be cruel."

"Cruel?"

She didn't speak.

There was a silence, a deep silence over the pool. Deep and dark and pervasive.

Nothing stirred.

When he heard her speak again it was almost in a low whisper, as if she had forgotten that he was there, as if she were completely alone, alone with herself and her inner thoughts.

"Cruel and mercilessly selfish. She's her father's daughter."

Then she stirred and saw his pale face.

"Kerry."

He was silent.

"Kerry," she said again.

"What is it, Marian?"

17

She crushed out her cigarette with her strong fingers and rose.

"I'm sorry," she said.

"For what?"

"I shouldn't have said that. I know how you feel about Licia."

"It was nothing," he said.

She shook her head. "You must forgive me."

"Nothing," he murmured.

She came closer to the pool's edge and leaned forward to him, her face tense and appealing. "I shouldn't have said what I said to you, Kerry."

"Marian."

"Please listen," she said.

"All right."

He could see tears in her eyes. "I never meant a word of it. Not a word."

"I know that, Marian."

"Please forgive me, I'm not myself today."

Her voice almost broke.

And before he could speak, she turned and went back into the darkness of the silent house.

Chapter

5

Like the others.

That's what Marian had said to him on the phone.

Licia has killed herself.

Killed herself.

Her self.

Like the others.

Yes, those were the words.

The others.

A mist came over his eyes and he hit the steering wheel with his fist again and again.

"Alicia," he whispered. "Why did you do what they did? Why?"

The car swerved and he gripped the wheel with his cold hands and drove on into the fierce sunlight.

"You always stood alone. Always alone."

Then he suddenly shouted.

"Why did you follow them, Alicia? Why?"

His voice echoed and was lost.

Only a flat stillness remained.

He began to tremble and he knew that he couldn't go on.

"Alicia," he whispered.

He stopped the car on the dusty shoulder of the road and just sat there looking through the clear windshield, out onto the deserted sandy beach.

. . . and from there to the low breaking waves

. . . to the shimmering horizon

. . . so vast and so endless

. . . so endless.

"Endless," he murmured.

There had been others.

And they had come to an end, a bitter and hopeless end.

He could not look anymore.

He closed his eyes.

There had been others, he thought, all during this dark and savage summer.

Three.

Ruth Cromwell and Nan Starrett.

They had choked their lives out together, sitting in a closed garage with the motor running, until they could breathe no more.

It was Alicia who told him about it.

He heard it first from her.

"Fools," she had said. "Such hopeless, spineless fools."

And then she had cried so much that he had to hold her close to him and comfort her. Then she became herself again, cool and self-possessed Alicia.

She didn't speak of it anymore.

Not one word.

And he stayed away from it, too.

But he didn't sleep nights.

Miriam Walker followed the other two, followed quietly.

She was the third.

The same way.

He remembered the newspaper reporters, the television people, the town meetings, the bitter questionings. They talked about the epidemic of teenage suicide in towns across the country. They said that suicide was the leading cause of death among young people. They quoted theories and statistics. But nobody could answer the question, Why?

Why?

Why is this happening to our children?

All questions and no good answers.

None that satisfied him.

"Why do people do that to themselves, Alicia?"

He was lying on the deck of her boat and looking up at the brilliant sky and talking to her.

It was two weeks after Miriam's funeral.

He had stood next to Alicia at the grave and her face was cold and white. Her hand tightly held his. Her shoulder was against his chest.

He felt that she had become a scared child at that moment. The moment the coffin was being lowered.

Scared.

And he had become her older brother. Strong and reassuring.

It was all there in the way she held on to his hand.

It was there.

He had wanted to bend over and kiss her hair, softly, gently.

Reassuringly.

"Why, Kerry?"

They had anchored off a wooded spit of land that led into the Sound. They were alone and no boats were within reach.

"Yes. It's a question that tortures me."

"Tortures?"

He sighed now. "Keeps me awake. Night after night."

"You should sleep," she said.

"As you do."

"As I do."

She was standing at the rail and looking out over the water. A tall, graceful figure.

"Well, Alicia?"

He waited for her to speak.

"Miriam was in love and it didn't work out," she finally said.

"That's a crock and you know it."

She smiled. "A good reason for killing yourself. Always was."

"Never was," he said.

She shook her head and her hair glinted in the sun.

"Wrong, Kerry. Unrequited love. Happens all through history. Especially to the romantics. And Miriam was a romantic."

"Cut it out," he said gently.

"She was."

He looked away from her to the endless horizon and then he heard her voice again, a cold, almost cruel voice.

"Miriam was a pure romantic. I should know. She was my good friend. For years. Love did her in, Kerry."

He turned back to her and his voice was hard.

"I said, cut it out. You're being ugly."

"Am I?"

"Yes."

"And it doesn't become me?" she said.

"It doesn't."

She laughed and the coldness of her laugh went through him.

"Think of Romeo and Juliet. They did themselves in, didn't they? Love, love, love," she said.

"Alicia."

"That's what makes the world fall apart, doesn't it? Love, love love."

He sat up and his face was tight with anger.

"All right, forget it. I was a jerk to ask," he said.

She flinched and looked down at him and suddenly a sad, almost childlike look came into her eyes. Childlike and so vulnerable.

"I'm sorry," she said.

He didn't speak.

"I'm in one of my sardonic moods," she said.

He still didn't speak.

"Sometimes I'm hard to be with. Isn't that so, Kerry?"

He nodded grimly. "It's so," he said.

"I really don't mean to be that way," she said.

"But you are."

She kept looking at him. "And now you're very angry with me."

"I am."

"And you'd . . . you'd like to . . ."

She stopped and didn't go on.

"Like to what?" he asked.

"To walk out of my life for good. Wouldn't you?"

"I would."

"Kerry."

He shook his head grimly. "That's exactly how I feel now."

"I don't believe you," she said.

"Believe me, Alicia."

"Why, Kerry? Why?"

"Because you're too hard to take."

"But I . . ."

"You are."

She silently sat down at his side and they both looked out at the water without speaking to each other for a long time.

Then he heard her voice. "Don't ever do that to me, Kerry."

He still was silent.

"Please, don't. Please bear with me. I need you so desperately," she said.

His lips were still shut in a tight line.

"Kerry."

She put her hand to his bare shoulder. It was cold.

Then he heard her say, "I'm scared. So terribly scared."

He slowly turned to her. "Of what, Alicia?" And his voice was soft.

But she didn't tell him.

It was only later on, much later on, that he found out.

But then it was too late.

Much too late.

Chapter

6

After Miriam Walker's death his father had phoned him from Rome. It was one in the morning and outside it had begun to rain, a slow, easy rain.

"Kerry?"

"Yes?"

"It's Dad."

"I know."

"Did I wake you?"

"No. I was sitting around reading."

"Oh," his father said. "Sorry if I waked you. I wanted to speak to you."

"You didn't wake me."

Kerry looked out through the open window at the dripping trees. It's going to be good for the grass, he thought. And then he said to himself, who really cares about the grass?

"How's the weather out there, Kerry?"

"Fine. Hot but fine."

"It's hot here. But it's much milder," his father said.

"So I've heard."

"Went to the Forum yesterday. Saw the ruins."

"How were they?" Kerry asked.

"I've seen them before. You know that."

"I guess I do."

"We were there with your mother. Years ago."

"Years ago," Kerry said.

A strange, unsettling thought came to him.

Who is my mother?

Where is she?

She's out on the coast and anchors a television news show.

That's right. She does.

That's all she cares about in this world. Her news show and its ratings.

Kerry, you don't know what a battle for life it is out here. You've no idea.

I really don't, Mom.

And he wanted to laugh but then he heard his father's voice again.

"Kerry?"

"Yes?"

"Think of it. Lucy has never been to Italy."

"Never?"

"Never out of the United States. Almost floored me when she told me."

"I guess you were surprised," Kerry said.

"I was. Floored me."

"How'd she like the Forum?"

"Fine. Just fine."

"Thrilled?"

"Yes. That's the word, Kerry. Thrilled."

"You're having a good time, Dad?"

"Yes."

"Lucy's having a good time?"

"Out of this world."

And then his father's voice became almost earnest and pleading. "Kerry, when you get to know her you're going to really like her. You will."

"I'm sure of it," Kerry said.

"Really like her."

"I'm looking forward to seeing more and more of her, Dad."

And he expected to hear his father say, you're putting me on again.

"Good, Son. Good."

There was a slight pause and Kerry looked out at the rain, the slow rain, and then his father spoke again.

"Kerry?"

"Yes?"

"I . . . I heard about those suicides."

"Oh."

"Your friends."

"Yes."

Again a slight pause.

"Kerry?"

"Well?"

"Are you all right?"

"Fine. I'm fine," Kerry said and looked out at the rain. Soon it will let up and go away, he thought.

"You're leveling with me?"

"Uh-huh."

"Lucy was saying maybe we should come on home and keep you company. How about it?"

"I'm okay."

"You see your other friends?"

"I do."

"And the house is not too lonely?"

"Not at all. I like it this way."

"You're not putting me on?"

"I'm leveling with you, Dad."

"Kerry?"

He waited.

"Kerry, maybe you ought to go out and visit with your mother."

"I'll think about it."

"She's up for an Emmy."

"Is she?"

"She might win it this time."

"That'd be great," Kerry said.

"Well, give it a thought."

"A thought?"

"About going out there."

"Oh, I will, Dad."

A pause and Kerry saw through the dripping leaves of the trees a flash of the headlights of a car out on the road and then the flash was gone and only the night remained. The night and the rain.

He heard his father's voice once more. "How's the weather?"

"Fine."

"No rain?"

"Very little."

"The grass in good shape?"

"Yes. I cut it regularly," Kerry said.

"Good. You need any money?"

"No. I'm in good shape."

"How's your friend, Alicia Kent?"

"Alicia? Okay."

"She's a very interesting girl," his father said.

"She is."

Kerry looked away from the rain and back to the walls of the room.

"Kerry?"

"Yes?"

"You sure you don't want me to come home?"

"I'm sure."

His father's voice rose just a bit. "And you're okay?"

"Yes. I told you I'm just fine."

"You told me."

There was a pause and then he heard, "I have a . . . a
. . . a great affection for you, Son."

Kerry felt a sudden surge of warm feeling for his father.

"I know that," he said gently.

"Kerry, listen to me."

"Well?"

"Maybe you should come out here. I'll book passage
soon as I hang up this phone. Just as soon as that."

Kerry shook his head. "No, Dad. I'll stay here."

"You sure?"

"Yes."

"Well . . . goodbye, Kerry."

Kerry didn't speak.

He heard the click and it made him feel sad and empty.

"Goodbye, Dad," he whispered.

Then he sat there a long while. He put out the lights and
let the darkness of the night envelop him.

Finally, he went up to his room.

Chapter

7

There was a small lake on the Kent estate and he was sitting on a stone bench looking out over the water when he saw a man emerge from the dark, silent trees and walk toward him.

He was tall and well-built and severe looking. His eyes were dark like Alicia's. And he carried himself the way she did.

Another patrician, Kerry thought.

The man came close and stopped.

"I'm Peter Kent," he said.

It was the first time Kerry had ever seen him.

"Oh."

"And you're Kerry." The man smiled.

"Yes."

"You're waiting for Alicia. To take her to a concert."

Kerry nodded silently.

"Do you mind if I sit with you a short while?"

"Not at all."

30

They sat, looking out over the placid lake. It was quiet and close to evening. The water glimmered with the dying sun.

"I find it very peaceful here. Especially at this time of day."

"It's very nice here," Kerry said.

They were silent again.

"You like Alicia," the man said suddenly in a quiet voice, his eyes studying Kerry.

Kerry didn't answer.

"And she likes you. That's evident to me." He took out a pack of cigarettes and offered them to Kerry.

Kerry shook his head. "Thanks, but I don't smoke."

Peter Kent smiles. "I shouldn't either. But unfortunately I do some things I shouldn't do."

"I guess we all do," Kerry said.

"Sometimes we get away with it and sometimes we don't. Isn't that so?"

"Yes."

"We get away with it. Especially when we're rich and powerful."

Kerry looked at the man. "Especially," he said.

"And you don't like it."

"I don't," Kerry said quietly.

"You're quite perceptive, as Alicia says you are. Perceptive and outspoken." Peter Kent nodded, his eyes dark upon Kerry, dark and searching. "As Alicia says," he murmured.

He lit his cigarette, the little wavering flame showing the line of his finely chiseled profile.

Then with his long patrician fingers he put away his silver lighter.

He smoked.

Kerry looked away from him to the lake.

A white bird, its whiteness shimmering in the faintly

glowing sky, settled down gracefully on the water and sat there, rocking gently.

But the trees surrounding the lake had darkened, the light rapidly fading from them, fading into a vast and heavy silence.

Kerry felt a deep sense of mystery and foreboding descending upon him. He felt an urge to get up and walk away from the man, out of Alicia's life, and away from the circle of darkening trees, a circle that seemed to be closing in on him.

But he sat there.

As if he had to.

As if a giant hand held him there.

Later, when he looked back in memory, he knew that the giant hand was that of inexorable fate. Fate and the subtle iron will of Peter Kent.

The man suddenly spoke, in a low and quiet voice.

"I have great plans for Alicia," he said.

Kerry stirred himself and listened.

"I'm trying to persuade her not to go on with her education."

"Why not?"

The man looked at him and smiled coldly. "Do you think she should?"

"If she wants to."

"You know her better than I do, Kerry. I'm only her father."

Kerry wondered if the man was mocking him.

I'm only her father.

"Does she really want to go to college, Kerry?"

"I don't think she knows herself. Not now."

"But what use would it all be? Only time wasted."

Kerry looked at the man's quiet and impassive face.

"Why wasted?" he asked.

"Well, she could spend it far better with me."

"With you?"

"Yes. I intend to hand over everything to her. Everything, Kerry."

"Why will you do that?"

"Why?"

"Yes."

The man snuffed out his cigarette on the stone bench, the tiny sparks flying upward and then falling to the dark ground underneath.

"Because Alicia is fully capable of taking it all on. More than any other human being I know."

"It could be," Kerry said.

"It is. There is no doubt in my mind."

"But why do you want to give it all up? You're not old and worn out. Why, Mr. Kent?"

"You're everything Alicia said you were," Peter Kent murmured and a glow came into the somber eyes.

Kerry waited.

He glanced away and then he became taut.

For there in the dimness of the trees, he thought he could make out the shadowy form of Alicia standing there, tall and silent, gazing intently at them.

Her face was white in the darkness.

He heard Peter Kent's voice.

"Why? Because I'd like to go on to other things."

Kerry turned back to him. "Such as?"

"Get into the political world. Perhaps run for the Senate."

Kerry looked back to the clustered trees and now he was sure she was there.

He felt that she could hear every word that they said. Felt it in his very bones. And yet they were speaking low to each other.

He turned back to the man.

"I believe you should let Alicia alone," he said.

33

"But I do."

Kerry looked fully at the man and shook his head. "You don't," he said. "You're always pressuring her."

The man's lips tightened into a thin line. "She's well able to handle my pressure."

Out on the lake the white bird still rocked gently, its whiteness the last glow of light on the rippling, darkening water.

Kerry suddenly spoke in a low and intense voice. "You're a selfish man, Mr. Kent. Maybe she doesn't care about your empire and your ambitions. Did you ever think of that?"

"Constantly."

Kerry went on. "Maybe deep inside of her she cares about other things. Things she's not even aware of. Why don't you let her alone and give her the time she needs to find out what she wants in this life?"

"Kerry," the man said. He slowly rose from his seat.
"Yes?"

Peter Kent paused before he spoke again.

"Let me give you a piece of advice. Listen carefully."
Kerry waited.

Then the man said in a low and quiet voice, "You're a very admirable young man."

"And?"

A bleak look came into the dark eyes. "Don't let Alicia break your heart."

"What?" Kerry whispered.

"She's quite good at that." And then he repeated, "Quite good."

Peter Kent turned and walked away from Kerry and into the darkness of the clustered trees.

When Kerry looked to where Alicia stood, he could no longer see her face or her form.

The night had come down upon her.

Chapter

8

In the end she did break my heart, Kerry thought, as he drove along the waterfront road, the sun striking fierce flashes of pure gold from the blue, placid water.

In the end she did.

Why, Alicia?

Why?

In the end we would have married.

Didn't you know that?

It was there.

In the years ahead of us.

Nothing would have broken us up.

Nothing.

Why, Alicia?

Why?

The great wrought-iron gates were open and he drove through them and up the long driveway to the huge house.

Gray and massive in the sunshine.

"It stands alone and dominates all about it, doesn't it, Kerry?" she had said.

"Yes, Alicia."

"A cold and ruthless dominance."

"Yes."

"Peter Kent built it that way. To let everybody around know that he is king of the hill."

"King."

"And I'm his princess," said Alicia.

"Do you like the house?"

"I hate it."

"No."

"Yes. Every brick of it. I'd burn it down if I could just get up the courage to do it."

"Alicia."

"I would."

But then at another time she had said, her dark eyes sparkling and her voice glowing, "I love the sense of power it gives me, Kerry. Just love it."

"Do you?"

"Yes. I get up in the morning and walk through the house and it sets me up for the day."

"I don't believe you," he said.

"Believe me. I was born for this life. And when you're born for it, you love it. Right from the start. Love it."

Kerry stopped the car and sat there gazing at the house.

And now you're dead, Alicia.

Dead.

And there's nothing to love anymore, is there?

Nothing.

And nothing to hate.

Is there, Alicia?

He looked at the two police cars parked by the wide steps and he slowly got out of his car.

One of the policemen came over to him.

"Nobody is allowed in," he said.

"Mrs. Kent sent for me," Kerry said.

"Your name?"

"Kerry Lanson."

"Okay."

He stood aside and let Kerry walk up the steps and into the house.

Chapter

9

He found Marian by the pool.

She was sitting alone.

She turned and rose and a terrified look came into her eyes when she saw him, a look he never forgot.

She moved back a step.

"Don't Kerry. Please don't."

She held her strong hands up defensively against him, as if she expected him to hit her.

He stared at her.

"Marian," he said gently.

Then her two hands fell limply to her sides.

"Oh, Kerry."

She hugged him close to her and began to cry.

"Licia, Licia," she moaned.

He didn't say anything.

"She had everything to live for. Everything. Why? Why, Kerry?"

He shook his head hopelessly. "Who knows?"

"Everything. She loved you, Kerry. She did."

"Yes," he murmured.

"And she knew how much you cared for her. She knew it."

He didn't speak.

"Why?" she said.

And he said again, dully and stupidly, "Who knows, Marian? Who knows?"

He put his arm around her and gently eased her back into her seat. Then he went over to another chair and drew it close to her.

And all the time he felt a dull heaviness in him.

Why don't I cry? he said to himself fiercely.

This is the time to do it.

Now.

Now when it is proper and decent.

Even the servants are crying.

There is not a tear in my eyes.

Not a one.

My voice is calm.

What is the matter with me?

What is Marian thinking? She expects me to cry. Everybody does.

What is it?

Deep down am I angry at Alicia for what she has done to me?

Angry?

At Alicia?

Done to me?

To me?

It's insane and cruel to even think that.

"Kerry?"

He turned to her.

"Yes, Marian," he said gently.

"Peter is in Japan. He doesn't know."

He stared at her.

"You mean no one has called him?"

She shook her head. "I'm the one who should. But I just can't do it. I can't, Kerry."

Her voice broke and she turned away from him and back to the pool, her tanned arms slack at her sides, her blonde head bent forward and down, her eyes vacant and anguished. The blue eyes that were always so calm and placid.

He felt a surge of pity for her.

"Easy, Marian. Easy," he murmured.

She shook her head hopelessly.

"I feel like a lost child," she said. "So lost. So utterly lost, Kerry. I can't seem to find . . . to find . . . find . . . peace . . . peace. . . ." Her voice trailed away into the silence.

All was still about them.

Only the lapping of the water could be heard.

Only that.

A quiet incessant sound.

Kerry sat listening to it and suddenly he felt that he could hear the distant laughing voice of Alicia as she swam alongside him in the pool.

Swimming easily and gracefully.

She was such a good swimmer, he thought.

Everything she did or tried was good.

No. It was better than good.

So much better.

She was a champion.

Matchless.

He kept looking at the water, no longer hearing her voice. It was gone, and suddenly the tears came to his eyes.

"Alicia," he whispered.

Then he roughly brushed away his tears with his big hand.

He closed his lips and kept looking at the water and listening to its sound.

He felt self-complete and alone.

As if time had stopped still.

Even life itself.

Alicia was still alive, sitting at his side, in a timeless world. Waiting to go back into the pool with him.

"I don't understand it," Marian said.

He stirred and turned to her.

She now spoke in a low and controlled voice. Her blue eyes were calm and yet in their depths the anguish remained.

"She didn't leave a message as the others did. Life being futile and useless. No. Just went ahead and did it. That's how Licia was. That's how she was."

Kerry shrugged silently.

She turned to him.

"You saw her last night. Didn't you, Kerry?"

"Yes," he said.

"And she . . . ?"

He shook his head silently.

"Not even a hint, Kerry?"

He didn't answer and the two didn't speak for a while.

"She was found in one of the garages," Marian suddenly said.

He felt a quiver run through him.

"Who found her?" Kerry asked.

"Henry. Mr. Kent's chauffeur."

"And then he told you?"

"Yes. He told me."

Her right hand gripped the arm of the chair.

Her face was pale and taut.

But her voice was still low and controlled.

"He went to get Peter's gray car and he opened the garage doors and there . . . there she was . . . slumped over the wheel."

"The motor running?" Kerry asked.

"A long time."

"She was . . . dead?"

"Yes."

"Nothing anyone could do for her?"

"Nothing."

"She was dead," Kerry said.

"Yes, Kerry. Yes."

Marian leaned back in her chair and closed her eyes.

He looked at the tired, slack face and he thought, I can see how you're going to look when you're old, Marian. When you're old.

And then he fought an urge to break down and cry like a beaten child.

Alicia will never get old, he said to himself.

Never.

Why?

Where's the justice of it all?

Where? For the love of God, where?

His hand closed tightly into a fist and he wanted to hit something, anything, just to smash it.

Marian spoke again, her eyes still closed.

"There was a book of poetry open at her side. A Keats poem. She must have been reading it."

" 'When I have fears that I may cease to be,' " Kerry said in a very low voice, as if speaking to himself.

Marian nodded. "That was the poem."

"It was one of her favorites."

"I know," Marian murmured.

" 'When I have fears that I . . .' " Kerry said.

And he thought he could hear Alicia's warm and intense voice as she read the opening lines of the poem.

Her eyes so gentle and soft when she looked up at him.

He covered his face with his hands and he heard Marian begin to cry again.

He wept silently.

Somewhere from the depths of the huge house the sound

42

of a telephone ringing came floating out to him. He listened to it and he felt an absurd impulse to get up, leave Marian, and go answer the phone. But he sat there. Laurie was in the house. She would hear it, too.

The ringing stopped.

He took out his handkerchief and wiped his eyes and face. Then he got up and went over to Marian.

She was no longer sobbing. Just a low moaning. "Her face was so . . . peaceful. Peaceful."

"I know," he said.

"How do you?" she asked.

She was now looking up sharply at him, her voice had hardened.

He didn't speak.

"I swear to you, Kerry. Peaceful. Why do you doubt me?"

"Easy, Marian. Easy," he said soothingly.

Her voice softened and broke. "Peaceful. You do believe me, don't you, Kerry?"

He nodded.

"Of course, Marian."

She reached up and held his hand. "I'm not myself, Kerry. Not myself."

"I know, Marian."

She slowly released his hand, her eyes still on his face.

"What can I say to Peter? What, Kerry?"

He patted her shoulder tenderly. "You must do it," he said.

She shook her head, almost violently. "I can't. I just can't."

"You'll do it. I'm sure you will," he said gently.

"No, Kerry. I'm at the end of my strength. It took all of it to face you. All of it."

"Marian, you . . ."

He sighed and didn't go on.

43

"Kerry?"

"Yes?"

"Would . . . Would you call him for me?"

He stared silently at her.

"Please. You were so close to her. Closer than I was. Closer even than her own father. She told me so, Kerry. She did."

He couldn't speak.

"I can't ask Laurie to do it. And I don't want the police to do it. I don't want to hurt him so."

Kerry was still silent.

"Will you . . . Will you do it for Alicia?"

He looked down at her tear-streaked face.

"She would have wanted it that way. You know that, Kerry."

He stroked her hair gently and then he turned and left her.

Chapter

10

"Mr. Kent is in conference but he will take your call."

"No," Kerry said. "Tell him I want to speak to him when he's alone."

"But . . ."

"Tell him that. Completely alone. No one in the room with him."

"I shall. It's Kerry Lanson calling."

"Yes."

"Please hold."

Alone, Kerry said to himself.

Alicia hated his conferences.

Despised them.

Rejected his world.

"No foundation all the way down the line, Kerry. They live on their own sweet planet and the rest of us down here on earth can go and die. No, it's not for me. Never."

And yet at another time and another mood . . .

"Why not, Kerry? I was born for it. It's my heritage. Why not take it? I'd be a fool and a graceless idiot not to."

Would she have gone into that world?

Would she?

Who will ever know now?

Then he heard the voice again. Crisp and cool. "Mr. Kent will be with you in a moment."

"Alone?"

"Yes. He's going into a private room."

"All right," Kerry said.

"Please be patient," the voice said.

"I will."

Then he waited until he heard Peter Kent's brisk but troubled voice. "Yes, Kerry?"

"It's about Alicia."

"Well?"

"I have terrible news for you, Mr. Kent."

He choked up for an instant and then he went on.

"That is why I wanted to speak to you alone."

"Alicia is . . . ?"

"Dead."

He could almost see the man go pale and grip the phone tight. But when the voice came to him again it was almost cold.

Toneless.

Metallic.

"How?"

"She committed suicide."

"Alicia?"

"Yes. She was found in the garage. The motor still running."

"Alicia," Peter Kent said again and this time his voice was weak and fumbling.

There was a long pause.

"Mr. Kent?"

"I'm here. I'm here. Alone. All alone."

Kerry felt his heart go out to the man, but the voice abruptly became metallic again.

"Tell Mrs. Kent I'll fly home immediately."

"I will."

"And thank you for calling, Kerry."

Then Kerry heard the click.

He found himself cold and shaking.

After a while he got up and left the room.

Chapter

11

Life is a dark corridor that leads to a dusty death.

A dark corridor.

He remembered Alicia saying those words to him. She was in one of her black moods at the time.

"Oh, come off it, Alicia."

She turned on him, her eyes flashing.

"Don't act superior to me, Kerry. I don't like it."

"I'm not acting superior to you. Just telling you stop talking and thinking like a . . . a . . ."

He didn't go on.

"Like what?"

"Nothing."

"Please tell me."

"Forget it."

"I want to hear it, Kerry."

The princess tone had come into her voice.

It grated on him.

"I said, forget it, Alicia."

"Tell me, Kerry. I insist that you do."

"Shove it."

She flinched as if he had struck her. "Kerry."

"Let me alone."

He got up and walked away from her and stood looking out at the lights of the boats on the Sound.

It was a warm summer night and they had been swimming and now they were back on the sand again.

She had been happy and they had been close to each other and now the mood set in. Until it became too much for him. She wouldn't let it go. Just wouldn't.

He kept looking out into the night, at the winking lights of the boats and then the sound of a laughing voice floated across the water to him, a woman's voice, pure and silvery, so full of the zest of life that it made him clench his hands. Then it lowered and faded and the silence came in again.

He stood there motionless, facing the sea and the night, his jaw set.

"You shouldn't treat me this way, Kerry."

She was now standing behind him and her voice was low and appealing. It sent a quiver through him. But he didn't turn to her.

"You shouldn't. It's very cruel," she insisted.

He didn't speak.

"Cruel. Knowing how much I care for you."

He sighed low.

"I have a right to express an opinion about life, don't I, Kerry?" she said.

"I guess so," he murmured.

"And about death, don't I?"

"No," he said and turned to her.

"What do you mean?"

"Alicia," he said.

"Yes?"

He paused and then he spoke. "There's been enough of

death in this town. You can feel it when you walk its streets. Forget it, will you? It's time already."

"Forget?"

"Yes. Yes."

"But I can't," she said.

"Then you must try harder. And you're not."

She shook her head. "I do try. All the time. But these were my friends."

"I know that," he said gently.

"They were your friends, too. They knew you and liked you. And you liked them. You did, Kerry."

"And I grieve for them," he said.

"I know you do."

"It's not that at all," he said.

"Then what is it?"

He didn't answer her.

Just stood there looking at her face.

The moon had just come out from behind a gray cloud and its pure light came down upon her.

He never forgot her face at that shining instant.

He stood there looking at her and he was sorry to the depths of his heart for his harshness to her.

He wanted to reach out and take her into his arms.

But he just stood there, motionless.

"What is it, Kerry?" she asked.

And he wanted to say to her, Alicia, when you get into one of your black moods and talk of death, I get scared.

Scared that I might somehow lose you.

That something terrible will happen to you.

"Alicia," he said.

"Yes?"

"All I really mean is that you should . . ." He didn't go on.

"Yes?"

He hesitated and then he spoke. "You've got a whole life ahead of you. It's all there. You've got everything going for you. Everything."

"Have I, Kerry?"

"Yes. Yes."

She looked away from him for an instant and then she said in a low and distant voice, "But I get very frightened."

"Of what?"

Now she looked directly up at him.

"That you'll leave me," she said.

"Alicia."

"Or that I'll leave you."

A cloud was gliding over the moon and Alicia's face was now in a softer light and it looked young and gentle to him. So very young and so vulnerable.

"Will you leave me?" he asked.

And then he repeated it.

"Will you, Alicia?"

"No," she said. "But it could be out of my hands."

"What do you mean by that?"

She didn't answer him.

He came closer to her.

"What, Alicia?"

"I'm scared that someone will kill me," she said.

He stared at her.

"Kill you?"

"Yes, Kerry."

"Why should anyone want to do that?" he asked.

She didn't speak.

"Who would?"

She shrugged. "I don't know. Just feel it."

"Oh, come off it, Alicia," he suddenly said and his voice was hard.

Yet underneath it all he felt a chill.

51

"I . . . I mean it, Kerry. If I take over the empire I'll become some sort of a celebrity. That's how it will work out," she said.

"So?"

"Some celebrities are killed in today's world. You know that."

"Alicia," he said.

"Yes?"

"Alicia, sometimes you talk like a six-year-old child."

This time she didn't get angry at him. Just looked up at him with wide, questioning eyes.

"Do I?" she asked.

"Yes. You sure do."

She smiled almost sadly and shrugged. "I guess I am a child then."

He nodded. "And the strangest person I ever met."

"Am I?" she asked.

"Yes, Alicia. There is no one like you. No one."

"Are you sure?"

"Yes."

She put her hand on his tentatively.

The moon had gone completely under the cloud and now there was no longer any light on her face.

Only a frail shadow.

He remembered that.

The shadow and the soft brown eyes with the last of the shine in them. The very last.

"But you like me with all that?" she asked in a low voice.

"With all that," he said.

He tightened his hand over hers.

"And you won't leave me, will you, Kerry?"

"No," he said.

"Promise?"

"Promise."

Then he put his arms about her and kissed her gently.

"Are you scared anymore?"

"No."

"You're not putting me on?"

"I'm not."

"All right," he said gently.

Then he heard the voice of laughter float over the water to him again, float from a great distance. And this time the laughter had changed its essence. Now it was harsh and cruel. Mocking. So clear. So distinct.

He stood there listening to it, and a great fear came into his heart.

"Let's go home," he said. "It's late."

They walked through the night to the car.

"I suddenly feel cold," she said, drawing closer to him. But the night was still warm.

Chapter

12

He drove into New York City and parked his car in a garage and then went down the block to the Four Seasons. He went inside and was stopped by the maitre d'.

"Yes?"

"Miz Sinclair's table."

"Evelyn Sinclair?"

"Yes."

"And you are?"

"Her guest," Kerry said.

"Come right along, please."

He was led inside and there was his mother sitting with a sleek, gray-haired man. They both rose when he came close.

"Kerry."

His mother held him to her and kissed him and then turned to the gray-haired man.

"He's as tall and handsome as I told you, John," she said.

"Yes, Evelyn. Favors you."

"Does he?"

"Very much," the man said.

She laughed quietly and kissed Kerry again. "He has the poise and maturity of one in his late twenties. You can see it readily. Isn't that so?"

"It certainly is," he agreed.

She released Kerry.

"Kerry, this is John Maltby, my executive producer."

"Glad to meet you."

Kerry shook hands with him and sat down.

His mother sipped her drink and put it down.

"Kerry is the quiet and steady one of our family, John. He had the look of a serious man when he was ten. Isn't that so, Kerry?"

"I wouldn't know," Kerry smiled.

But he remembered with a sharp pang that it was then the trouble started between his father and mother.

The cold, quiet arguments. Cold, controlled, but devastating. Two people slowly stripping each other naked before him, and never being aware of it. Their manners were so civilized and impeccable.

She patted his hand. "We're in for the day," she said.

"Just for the day," Maltby smiled.

"We're taking the five o'clock out of here to the coast."

"Oh." Kerry was disappointed but he didn't show it.

"I didn't want to miss the chance of seeing you," his mother said. "It was nice of you to come on short notice. Sweet of you, Kerry."

"It was," Maltby said.

"I wanted to see you, too, Mom," Kerry said. "I'm glad you called."

"Lucky I was able to catch you."

"Yes."

"I called a few times but you were out. No answer."

"I've been around," Kerry said.

"Been swimming a lot? The weather's been perfect for it, I understand."

Kerry nodded silently.

"We've had a lot of rain. My garden is a disaster," she said.

"I've been swimming," Kerry said.

His voice trembled just a bit and he caught himself and smiled.

"Not alone, I'm sure," Maltby smiled.

"No," Kerry said.

"A blonde mermaid at his side." His mother laughed softly and Maltby laughed with her. "Maybe two," he said.

His mother shook her head. "No, John. One. Kerry always went with one at a time. Isn't that so, Kerry?"

"Only one," Kerry said.

Kerry looked at them and wondered what Alicia would have thought of his mother.

Alicia could be harsh and devastating when she wanted to.

"You always loved swimming," his mother said and turned to Maltby. "He's an excellent swimmer. Superb. Could have won many medals but he doesn't believe in competition. Just swims for the sheer fun of it. Isn't that so, Kerry?"

"I guess that's right."

"His father was the champion. Gold medal in the Olympics. But he always said that Kerry was the better swimmer."

"He's built like a swimmer," Maltby said approvingly.

"His father's build. Wide shoulders and slim hips. Takes after him there. But only in that aspect."

She finished her drink with one swallow and then asked, "Where is he these days?"

Her voice was quite casual but her eyes were on him.

"Rome and Venice," Kerry said.

"Venice," she said. "Yes. I remember Venice."

Her eyes hardened and she abruptly motioned the waiter to come over to them. "We're ready now," she said in a crisp voice.

Kerry sat back and studied her as she ordered.

You're as young and as attractive as ever, he thought to himself.

You've aged but a few years.

Life seems to skim over you.

Alicia would have looked as young as you do at your age.

I'm sure of that.

But her eyes would have been softer.

And more loving.

Yes, Mother. More loving.

You're getting what you want out of life, aren't you?

And what's wrong with that?

And yet . . .

And yet I think you're losing out.

All the way.

All the rotten way, dear Mother.

"Shall I order for you, Kerry? I know what you like," she said.

"Something light. I'm not in the mood to eat much lately."

She looked alertly up at him. "Anything wrong?"

"No, Mom. Nothing at all."

"Are you sure?"

"Positive."

She picked up the menu again. "All right," she said.

Maltby leaned over and patted Kerry on the shoulder. "It's girl trouble, isn't it?" he said in a fatherly voice.

"Yes."

Maltby chuckled. "It will straighten out. It always does."

57

Then he and Kerry laughed but all the time his mother was looking at him. And it was then that he wanted to reach out and take her hand, and hold it tightly.

Just as he had held Alicia's.

To hold her hand and to speak to her.

Mom, I came in to see you and to talk to you.

Alone.

Just the two of us.

Why did you bring him along?

Why?

You're my mother. Shouldn't a fellow have the chance to open up his heart to his mother?

Shouldn't he?

Especially when it pains so much.

Night and day.

Without letup.

He wanted to tell her how hard life was getting for him.

Making it almost impossible to go on.

Mom?

There's nobody to turn to anymore.

Nobody.

"Kerry?" she said.

"Yes?"

"Did you know Alicia Kent?"

He stared at her. "Who?"

"Alicia Kent. The heiress who just committed suicide."

"Oh."

"It's been all over television. And in the newspapers," she continued.

Kerry was silent.

"Did you, Kerry?" Maltby asked.

Kerry looked at him. "Very slightly," he said.

"Oh, that's a shame," Maltby murmured.

"Why?"

"Well, we're planning to do a series on teenage suicide."

"And?"

"We thought you could give us some inside information," his mother said.

"Inside?"

She nodded. "Yes. We have all our research in. But the personal life is what we're after. How she really was. What you knew of her. That's always great human material."

"Grabs the viewer by the gut," Kerry said.

"That's it, Kerry. That's it exactly," Maltby said, his eyes lighting up.

"But you say you weren't close to her," his mother said.

"I wasn't."

"Do you know people who could help us? We want to feature Alicia Kent," his mother went on.

Kerry shook his head.

"We traveled in different circles," he said quietly.

There was a slight silence.

His mother sipped her second drink, savoring it, and then put down the glass. "A friend of ours who's in the know passed on the information that a trace of a drug was found in the body."

Kerry's face whitened.

"The officials, of course, will deny it, Kerry," she added.

"It's all very, very confidential," Maltby said.

"Peter Kent will use his power to suppress that information. It will never see daylight," she said.

Kerry looked silently at the two.

Maltby spoke first. "Do you think you could find out for us, Kerry? Say from one of her close friends? You might be able to do that for your mother?"

His mother leaned forward to him. "I have a good chance to win an Emmy with this show, Kerry. A really good one. It's just what I need for my career now."

"Evelyn Sinclair is on her way up," Maltby said. "Who knows how high she can go after this one?"

"John is right, Kerry," she said, a glow in her eyes.

Kerry clenched his hands under the table and then slowly opened them.

"Alicia Kent never touched a drug," he said in a flat voice.

They both looked at him.

"How do you know?" Maltby asked.

"I know it. Better than anybody else in this world."

"But, Kerry," Maltby said. "You just told us you never knew Alicia Kent."

"I did."

"But how do you . . . ?"

"John," Kerry's mother cut in. "Let's not go on with this."

He turned to her.

"What do you mean?"

"Let's forget the whole thing," she said.

He stared at her.

"Forget?"

"We won't use Alicia Kent at all."

"What?"

"We have enough material without her."

There were beads of perspiration on Maltby's forehead. He turned pleadingly to Kerry and then back to her.

"But the show was planned around Kent. That's the centerpiece of it all. The centerpiece, Evelyn."

"I know."

"It will just be another show. Like everyone else's."

"That's how the cookie crumbles, John."

He raised his hand helplessly to her. "Evelyn."

She shook her head firmly. "Alicia Kent is out of the show. Not even a mention of her."

"Not even that?"

"Yes."

He looked at her and sighed. "Whatever you say, Evelyn."

"Thanks, John."

Then she turned to Kerry with a smile, but her face was pale and drawn. "Let's eat. Shall we?"

"Yes," Kerry murmured.

For an instant, his mother looked old and weak to him. He wanted to reach out and comfort her.

But he just sat there.

And then the instant was gone.

Her face was young, cold, and alert again.

She ordered another round of drinks and this time he drank with them.

They talked and ate their meal and it was all very pleasant and then at the end Kerry got up and kissed his mother and shook hands with Maltby.

"Very good to meet you, Mr. Maltby."

"Call me John."

Kerry smiled. "John."

"That's better."

"Kerry," his mother said. "You must promise me that you'll come out and stay with me for a while."

"Yes, Mom."

"Make it soon."

"Okay."

"Promise?"

"Promise."

And he remembered Alicia saying, on the beach that night, "Promise?"

Her eyes as she looked up at him, so desperately appealing.

He remembered with a sharp pang his reply.

"Promise."

And he wanted to shout so that the whole noisy, chattering restaurant would hear him.

What good on earth are promises? Tell me, what good? It's all a corridor. A dark corridor. That's all it is. Nothing else. She was right. Alicia was right. All the way down the line. Life is nothing but a corridor that leads to death. Vile, dusty death. Can't you see it? Are you blind? Or is that why all of you drink so much? Is that why? Answer me, Mother. Answer me.

But he didn't shout.

He didn't even speak.

He just smiled and left them.

Chapter

13

He couldn't sleep that night so he got up and went down to the pool and swam for a while. Then he got out and dried himself and sat down on one of the chairs.

Brooding. Ever brooding.

"Drugs?"

"Yes, Alicia."

"Why do you ask?"

"Just came to me."

"There must be a reason."

"No reason."

She laughed softly and pressed his arm.

They were lying on her boat looking up at the gray, dismal sky. It looked like rain but the day was hot and they didn't mind if it did rain.

"No, Kerry," she said. "I don't go for them."

"Some of our crowd do."

"I know that."

"But not you?" he asked.

"Not me."

"Why not?"

"Just don't go for it. That's why not."

They were silent and then he spoke again. "I tried it once and it was no dice. So that was the end of it for me."

"Never again?"

"Never."

"You're your own man when it comes to the important things, aren't you?"

"I try to be," he said quietly.

She laughed softly. "It's sometimes hard to tell when a friend is on the stuff, Kerry. You know that, don't you?"

"I wouldn't know."

"Well, I would. Nan Starrett was into them for a long time and she fooled everybody. But not me. It's really hard to tell with some people."

He turned and looked long at her. "And it would be hard to tell with you?"

She nodded but her eyes twinkled. "I'm great at covering up things I want to. I'm a past master at that."

"So?"

And the twinkle was gone from her dark eyes. "So let's drop the subject. It's going to put me in one of my moods."

"Will it?"

"Definitely."

"Then let's drop it," he said.

"Thanks."

She laughed softly again.

But he had noticed that her hands trembled just a bit while she spoke of Nan Starrett. And now as he sat on the chair in the darkness of the night, he thought of that and it would give him no rest.

The trembling hands.

Those long, tapered fingers shaking.

And a question rose up from the depths of his being.

Was she lying to me, he asked.

Was she?

Alicia.

Alicia.

He suddenly stood up and called out into the night.

"Alicia, Alicia."

His voice rose against the harsh darkness.

"Where are you? Where?"

His cry echoed out.

Then all became silence again.

He stood there feeling the night beginning to close in on him and he began to shiver. So he sat down on the chair and covered himself.

But the shivering wouldn't stop.

Chapter

14

Then he said to himself, I'd better watch out.
  I'd better.
  I'm standing at the threshold of the dark corridor.
  I'd better not step over it.
  Or I'll end up as she did.
  She and the others before her.

Chapter

15

In the morning there was a special delivery letter from his father and in the envelope was an airline ticket.

He read the brief note.

Kerry, I've just learned of Alicia Kent's suicide and funeral. I want you here. I'm in Spoleto and will be here for a while. I repeat, I want you here. You've got five days to prepare and to get on that plane. I repeat, I want you here.

Dad.

Kerry put the envelope on the table.
The phone rang.
He picked it up.
"Yes?"
"Kerry?"
It was Peter Kent.
"Yes, Mr. Kent."
"I'd like to see you."

The voice was cold and peremptory.

"All right. When?"

"Could you come over this afternoon?"

"Yes."

"Make it at three."

"Yes, Mr. Kent."

"Goodbye, Kerry."

"Goodbye."

Kerry's voice faded into the silence.

He put down the phone and stood there thinking. And it was then that he felt that someone was standing in the sunlit garden looking at the house.

With piercing cold eyes.

He went slowly out to the terrace and as he did he saw a figure slide away from behind one of the old gnarled oak trees and disappear into the shade.

He called out, but there was no answer.

Only the morning silence.

Chapter

16

While he was standing outside Peter Kent's study, Laurie Kent came down the long, shadowy hall and stopped by him.

"Hello, Kerry."

"Laurie."

She smiled at him and it was only then that he realized how much she looked like her mother. A much younger version. She had Marian Kent's blonde hair and her stocky, athletic figure. The same blue, calm eyes.

But now the eyes were vague, tentative and questioning.

"Seeing father?" she asked.

"Yes."

"He doesn't say much these days."

"I guess he doesn't."

"The house is not the same with Alicia gone," Laurie said.

Kerry was silent.

"She lit it up. And now she's gone."

"Yes," Kerry murmured.

"But there's nothing to do but go on with life. Isn't that so?"

"Yes, Laurie."

She looked directly into his eyes. "We have to get over it. There's nothing else."

"Nothing else," he echoed.

And he had the strange and uneasy feeling that she had been waiting in the house for him. He knew that she always went out to the golf course at this hour. Religiously.

Alicia had laughed at Laurie for desperately wanting to be a golf pro and compete in tournaments. To be an even better player than her mother was.

"Laurie is a girl of world ambition, Kerry."

"Alicia."

"A limited mind and a limited soul."

"Alicia, cut it out. You're showing me your ugly side again. And I'm tired of it."

"Are you?"

"Yes."

And he was turning away from her when she held her hand out to him and stopped him. "I'm sorry, Kerry."

"You're not."

"Sometimes I say those things. Just say them. I can't seem to help myself."

"You can if you tried to be decent."

"I'm not decent?"

"Not then, Alicia."

"Oh . . . Please forgive me, Kerry."

He sighed. "All right. Let's drop it."

"It's dropped. I do care for Laurie. Care for her a lot."

"Okay."

"You must believe that. She's like a sister to me," she said.

"I do believe you."

"A sister. I never had one. Or a brother. I'm alone, Kerry. All alone."

"So am I."

Now standing in the long hall, he heard again Laurie's voice. Yet Alicia still hovered in his memory.

"Kerry?"

He looked down at her and saw her again.

"I've been talking to you, Kerry, and you haven't been listening. There was a faraway look in your eyes."

"Oh. I'm sorry, Laurie."

"A sad look. You were thinking of Alicia, weren't you?"

He nodded silently.

"You've got to stop that, Kerry."

"I know."

"We've all got to go on. But I've said that already, haven't I?" she said.

"Yes."

"There's no other way, is there?"

"No."

"And you're going to try hard?"

He nodded. "Yes, Laurie."

She kept looking at him, and then she said in a soft voice, "I've always liked you, Kerry. A lot. You knew that, didn't you?"

He shook his head. "I didn't, Laurie."

Her face was flushed, and her eyes were upon him. "Well, I do. You don't mind my saying this to you now?"

"Not at all, Laurie."

"Are you sure?"

"Yes."

She drew a little closer to him. "Would you like us to see each other?"

And for a strange, eerie instant, he had the sensation that Alicia was standing near them and laughing.

He could almost hear the soft, mocking laughter.

71

"Us, Laurie?"

"Yes, Kerry. I know I'd like it very much."

Her body fragrance was soft and penetrating. "Very much," she murmured.

He was about to speak when he saw down at the end of the hall, at its very end, the figure of Marian Kent, standing watching them. Silently watching them.

The sun was glinting on her blonde hair but the rest of the figure was in shadow.

Her eyes seemed to gleam coldly, even from that distance.

Laurie turned and saw her mother and whitened.

Then she abruptly left him, without saying a word.

And he thought again he could hear Alicia's ghostly laughter.

Chapter

17

"I warned you that she would break your heart. But you wouldn't listen."

Kerry sat across from the man but he didn't speak.

"She broke mine. That's certainly true. Broke it and left me with nothing to go on. Nothing."

His eyes were bleak.

His face gaunt.

The lips now grimly shut.

Gray and bloodless.

Peter Kent had aged since Kerry saw him last. Had aged in a few short days and Kerry, looking at him, felt a great compassion and he wanted to say something.

But there was nothing to say.

The two sat in a huge, oak-paneled room and all was quiet about them.

Severely quiet.

Not a sound was heard in the entire house.

Nor from outside it.

The long windows of the study went from floor to high

ceiling and they were shut, the curtains drawn across them.

Kerry thought of Alicia sitting here and discussing the affairs of the Kent empire with her father. Peter Kent sitting across the vast oak desk in his roomy leather chair, an austere look on his patrician face.

Alicia had laughed when she told him of those discussions.

"He's so serious, Kerry. And he's convinced that I'm a genius. And unfortunately that's what I am. But it's all such trivia and nonsense. Like playing with toys. Really, Kerry. I feel so above it all. Why does he bother with it? Why?"

"What are you smiling at, Kerry?" Peter Kent asked.

"Smiling?"

"Yes."

"I'm sorry. I didn't realize it," he said.

"Is this a time to smile? Is it?"

Kerry didn't answer.

The man sat there nervously tapping his long fingers on the desk and gazing at Kerry, his eyes glowering, and then suddenly he leaned forward, his face intense and his voice harsh.

"You are a young fool. A cruel one."

"What?"

Peter Kent's head nodded again and then he suddenly lashed out at Kerry. "You're all young fools. All of you. Young and heartless. You're a worthless generation. Cowardly. A generation of cowards. You don't face life. You run away from it. Away from life into easy death. Young, young fools."

Kerry was silent.

"And yet you, Kerry, are even more than that."

"What do you mean?"

"You had Alicia's life in your hands and you smashed it."

"I?"

"Yes, you. You and your selfish, self-centered, self-indulgent . . . your . . . your cruel and heartless . . . heart . . ." He choked up and stopped speaking.

There were cold, gleaming drops of perspiration on his white forehead. He looked away from Kerry to the curtained window, his lips quivering.

Kerry kept staring at the man and he felt a chill go over him.

He's coming apart at the seams, Kerry thought, and it's terrible to see it.

Terrible and frightening.

Will this happen to me?

Is this happening to me?

Is it?

Alicia, why did you do it?

Why?

Peter Kent turned away from the window and back to Kerry and when he spoke again, his voice was icy and controlled. "How old are you, Kerry?"

"Old? You know that."

"Tell me. Lie to me."

"Lie?"

"Yes. Just as you do when you go into a bar. When you . . ."

"I don't know what you're talking about," Kerry cut in.

The man nodded his head grimly.

"Oh, yes you do. For you are liars, all of you. Even Alicia was a liar. You're a generation of liars." His voice rose. "You show one face to the world and the other is a mask. Masks beneath masks. Who will ever find the truth in you? Who in this world ever can?"

"Alicia was never a liar," Kerry said fiercely. "Never was."

"Don't tell me about my daughter."

"I don't want you talking that way about Alicia," Kerry

said. "Whether she was your daughter or not. I won't sit here and listen to it."

Peter Kent didn't speak.

He turned his face away from Kerry.

The two sat there, a great distance separating them.

Then the man suddenly beat his fist on the desk and rose.

"Let's get out of here," he said. "I can't stand this confining space any longer. Get out into the air. What I have to say to you should be said there. Where I can breathe again."

Kerry remained in his chair.

The man came to him and stood over him.

"Come with me. Do you hear!"

"All right," Kerry muttered.

He got up and followed Peter Kent out of the room and then out of the silent, gray house and into the shining day.

The sky above them was blue and clear and vast.

The air glowed.

It's the kind of day that Alicia always loved, Kerry thought.

It's so good to be alive, Kerry. So very good.

Yes, Alicia.

I feel I could live forever. Don't you?

Forever, Alicia.

Just the two of us.

Yes.

Peter Kent walked with long strides up the grassy knoll until they reached its broad green top.

Let's go out on the boat, Kerry. It's just the day for it, she had said.

Those days are gone, Alicia.

Gone forever.

Peter Kent paused and looked back at the huge, glowing mansion, the windows flaring in the strong sun.

All about the two was serene and beautiful, pulsing with colorful life.

"I've come to hate that house," he said quietly.

Kerry was silent.

"I built it for Alicia. Built it with great love and care."

And now you hate it, Kerry thought with an ache in his heart.

Why is love so fragile?

So easily destroyed.

Why?

Then he heard the man speak again.

"Alicia hated it, too, didn't she?"

"Alicia?"

"Yes."

"I couldn't say."

"Don't lie to me, young man."

"I am not lying."

"You are. You know she did."

Kerry turned and fully faced the man. "I'm telling you the truth. Alicia would hate the house one day and love it the next. That was the way with many things in her life. You know that better than I do, Mr. Kent."

Peter Kent shook his head grimly. "I know nothing about her. Nothing at all. I find that out now. Find it out so very bitterly."

He paused and then continued in a low voice. "It's as if she never lived in my house. Never."

He turned wearily away from Kerry and then slowly sank down on the ground and set his back against the trunk of a tree that stood alone on the knoll.

A soft breeze blew over them and Kerry just stood there watching the rippling green grass. Then he turned and looked down at the house and from there to the garage buildings.

And he thought of Alicia lying dead in the sleek, silver-gray car.

The book of Keats' poems lying at her side.

"When I have fears that I may cease to be . . ."

Her lips open, whispering the words.

"When I have fears . . ."

Then Death put his hand to her lips and shut off her breath, the book of poems falling to her side.

Alicia.

He heard Peter Kent speak again. This time his voice was low and brooding. "Kerry," he said.

"Yes?"

"Kerry, you alone knew her and she listened to you. All the time it was you and only you." He paused and then went on. "Nobody else could influence her but you. You held her life in your hands and you killed her."

"Killed her? Alicia?"

"Yes, Kerry. As if you had put a gun to her head and pulled the trigger."

Kerry stared at the man and couldn't speak.

"You introduced her to drugs, didn't you?"

"What?"

"No one else could do that to her. No one but you. No one else."

"I don't know what you're talking about," Kerry said angrily.

"Oh, you do, young man. You certainly do."

He slowly rose and then faced Kerry.

"She had traces of a drug in her system when she died. And you helped put it there."

Kerry shook his head fiercely. "No. That's not so at all."

"What time did you leave her that night?"

"Time?"

"Yes. Tell me," Peter Kent demanded.

"I don't know. Somewhere between twelve and one."

"You left her off at the house, didn't you?"

"No."

"What do you mean?"

"Alicia drove her car. She dropped me off at my house and then she went on."

"She was very depressed, wasn't she?"

"Depressed? No. Not at all."

"She was. The reaction to the drug had set in. Isn't that so? The down feeling? The feeling that life is worthless and hopeless."

"I can't follow you," Kerry said bitterly.

"She came home. Went to her room and then sometime during the night she decided to go down to the garage and . . . and . . ." He turned away and didn't go on.

"Mr. Kent," Kerry said. "Alicia and I had nothing to do with drugs. Nothing. You must believe me."

"I don't."

"I left Alicia in a good mood. She was happy."

"Of course."

"I'm telling you the truth," Kerry insisted.

"Beyond any doubt."

"Why don't you believe me?"

"Because you're a liar."

"Mr. Kent, I . . ." And Kerry stopped speaking and looked hopelessly into the man's cold face.

"You made a date for the next day, I suppose."

"Yes. That's exactly what happened."

"You lie," Peter Kent said in a hard voice. "Laurie saw Alicia before she went to her room."

"Laurie?"

"Yes. And she says that Alicia was very pale and very depressed."

"Laurie is mistaken."

"I don't think so."

"She is, I tell you," Kerry protested.

Peter Kent shook his head grimly.

"No. She's not. Alicia was shaking and there was a wild look in her eyes. Laurie tried to help her but she screamed at Laurie and ran into her room. Ran in and locked the door. The next morning, the door was wide open and Alicia was dead in the garage."

"I tell you Alicia left me feeling happy and looking forward to our seeing each other the next day," Kerry said.

"Looking forward to her death, you mean."

"No. Laurie is all wrong."

"She is not."

"I left Alicia and her last words to me were . . ."

"Enough," Peter Kent cut in savagely, his voice rising. "I don't want to hear any more."

"But . . ."

"Enough. All I know is that you are my daughter's murderer. That's how I look upon you."

"No. You must hear me out. You must." Kerry's voice rose.

The man shook his head, his face tight and stern. A fierce glow lay deep in the dark eyes. "The trial is over," he said.

"Trial?"

"You stand convicted."

Kerry stared at the man, a cold chill settling over him. His hands shook.

There was a silence.

A deep, brooding silence.

Even the leaves of the tree hung still.

"Have you gone mad?" Kerry finally said.

"Yes. And it is you who have made me so."

The man's lips were bloodless.

The fierce eyes piercing into Kerry.

Kerry moved closer.

"Mr. Kent," he said. "Please listen to me. I know all you've been through and . . . and . . . I . . ."

80

He kept looking at the eyes and his voice stopped and died.

Then he heard.

"I said you are convicted, didn't I?"

"But . . ."

"There is nothing more to say."

Peter Kent turned abruptly and began to walk away from Kerry. And then suddenly he stopped.

He swung around.

His voice rang out against the silent day.

"I'm going to make you pay for her death. I will, Kerry. Even with your life if I can do it."

His voice lowered, almost to a whisper, yet Kerry could hear every word.

"And I can. Yes, murderer. I can do it."

Then he started down the hill to the gray, somber house.

"You're wrong," Kerry shouted after him. "All wrong."

But the dark, vengeful figure never turned.

Chapter

18

He took the airline ticket out of the envelope and looked at it.

Maybe I should listen to my father and go over to Spoleto.

Get out of here.

Why should I stay on?

Why?

I'll go over there and knock around with Dad and his wife for a while and we'll all have a good time.

She's okay.

I'll get along with her.

He's okay.

I'll get along with him.

So what's keeping me here?

I can't sleep anymore.

I don't eat much.

I'll start to drink.

That's what I'll do if I stay on.

I will.

I know I will.

I'll just crack up.

Just like her father.

That's what Alicia has done to him.

And she'll do the same to me.

I know it.

And I'll start hating Alicia.

No.

Not that.

Please, God, keep me from that.

Anything but that.

He looked out into the dark night a long time and then he sighed and slowly put the ticket back into the envelope and placed the envelope back into the drawer.

What's the use? he said to himself wearily.

I've got to stay here.

Here.

With Alicia.

I can't go on until I find out the truth.

Even if it means my life.

Even if at the end I get killed or kill myself.

But I've got to stay.

On the threshold of the dark corridor.

Chapter

19

He was sitting on the dock waiting for Becky Cobb to come in with her boat. And he found himself thinking of Alicia.

He leaned his head against an old weathered post and closed his eyes, the sun warm and soothing upon him, a gentle sea breeze playing with strands of his hair.

He felt Alicia's long tapering fingers softly touching his forehead.

Softly.

Ever so softly.

Kerry?

Yes, Alicia?

There are times when I feel that you don't trust me.

Trust you? What do you mean?

You get a look in your eyes. A strange, almost sad look, Kerry.

Sad?

Yes.

And?

And I can sense that you feel that I am not what you think
I am.

Come again?

Just what I said.

And what do I think you are, Alicia?

You tell me.

Shall I?

Yes.

The truth?

Please, Kerry.

All right. Well, Alicia, I sometimes feel that you hide
things from me.

For example?

I don't know.

Come on. Stop kidding around.

I'm not, Alicia.

Tell me.

No. I really mean it. There are times when I feel that I
don't know you at all. The real you. I look at you and I feel
that I'm looking at a . . . a . . .

Yes?

A . . . a sphinx.

A what?

I mean it. There are times when I feel there's another
Alicia, the true one, and I . . .

Another Alicia, no less.

Yes.

And the true Alicia is a sphinx. Is that it?

Well, I . . .

And you've been kissing the cold, stone lips of a sphinx?

Alicia.

How does it feel, kissing stone lips?

Alicia, cut it out.

Tell me.

You're laughing and I'm trying to be serious.

Are you?

Alicia.

He sat there, his eyes still closed but a soft smile on his lips, still listening to Alicia's melodic laugh.

Then he heard the voice.

"What's so funny, Kerry?"

He opened his eyes and saw Becky Cobb smiling down at him.

"Oh."

"What is it?"

He stood up and smiled at her. "Nothing, Becky. Really nothing. I've been waiting for you."

"Have you?"

She seemed pleased.

"Uh-huh. You have a good sail?" he asked.

"Yes."

"You hungry?"

"Why?"

"Well, I wondered if you would have lunch with me?"

She laughed gently. "I'm hungry, Kerry."

"Good. Any place in particular?"

"You pick it."

"How about the Cameo?"

She looked quietly at him. "That was Alicia's favorite place, wasn't it?"

He nodded. "Yes," he said softly. "It was."

"It's good enough for me."

He pointed to the boat in the slip.

"All set with it, or do you want me to help?"

She shook her head. "All taken care of, Kerry."

"Let's go then."

"Okay."

She was almost as tall as Alicia, slender and tall, and she had light brown hair, gentle features, and hazel eyes.

He had always liked her. He had gone out with her a few

times and he saw that she liked him a lot, but then he met Alicia.

"I'll take my car and you take yours, Becky. Okay?"

"Sure."

He followed her to the parking lot and watched her get into her gray Porsche and then he went over to his car.

There was a small, oblong piece of white paper stuck under the windshield wiper. He lifted the wiper blade and took the paper from under it.

He read the word written on it.

Murderer.

He let the paper fall to the pebbled ground.

It lay there, white in the sun.

Then he got in and started his car, his face gray and taut.

Chapter

20

They sat alone at a table that overlooked the water. All during the meal he kept looking at the sails, far out, his eyes distant and sad.

"Kerry?"

He turned to her. "Yes, Becky?"

"You haven't been good company."

"What?"

She smiled gently at him.

"It's been a pretty silent meal."

"Oh. I'm sorry, Becky. I didn't realize it."

"That's all right."

"It isn't. I asked you to lunch and then I . . ."

He shrugged and was silent.

She leaned forward and touched his hand. "What is it? Alicia?"

He nodded. "Yes."

He looked away from her and back to the reach of blue water, serene and shining.

He heard Becky speak again.

"You've got to forget and go on, Kerry."

He remembered Laurie using the exact words.

"I know, Becky," he said. He turned back to her. "I know all that."

His voice was weary.

"And yet it's awfully hard, isn't it, Kerry?" she said.

He nodded but didn't speak.

She leaned forward to him.

"You don't look well, Kerry. I can see it's starting to get to you. You shouldn't let it. I know I'm saying words but it's the truth."

"It's the truth, Becky," he said.

"So?"

"So nothing. I can't help myself."

"You must. For example, we shouldn't be sitting here."

"Why not?"

"I tried to remind you that this was Alicia's favorite place."

"You did."

"Yet you come here. You seem to want to hurt yourself. And that's not good. Not good at all."

And then when he didn't speak, she leaned forward again to him and spoke in a low voice, her eyes gentle.

"You must free yourself from Alicia. Or you'll be in great trouble, Kerry."

He looked away from her.

I'll never free myself, Becky. I know that now. I'll go down the same way she did. Alicia will drag me down with her.

I know that now.

"Kerry."

"Yes?"

"You asked me to have lunch with you. You were waiting for me at the dock. Why?"

He hesitated.

"Well?"

"I wanted to talk to you about Alicia."

"Oh."

And he could see her eyes darken, her lips tighten just a bit.

But he went on.

"You knew her much longer than I did, Becky."

She nodded. "I grew up with her."

"You were always friends."

"Yes. We were."

"You went out together a lot."

Her eyes had become cold, her manner wary. "We did. What are you driving at, Kerry? I wish you'd let it alone."

"I can't," he said.

"Why not?"

"I just can't."

They looked silently at each other.

Then he spoke again. "You were close to her," he said.

Becky shook her head. "Nobody was ever close to Alicia. Nobody but you, Kerry."

And he remembered Peter Kent saying bitterly to him, You knew her better than I did. Nobody knew her better than you.

"Becky."

"Yes?"

"Did Alicia ever use drugs?"

She sat back and stared at him.

"What?" she said.

"I've got to know. You must tell me."

"I said you were closer to her than anybody else. Why do you ask me such a question? Why?"

He leaned forward to her. "Please, Becky. If you know, tell me one way or another."

"I said, forget Alicia."

"But . . ."

"Forget her." She slowly rose from her seat.

"No, Becky. You must tell me."

He rose and faced her.

"Kerry."

"You must," he said.

"People are looking at us. Let's get out of here."

"Becky."

"I'm leaving you, Kerry. Now."

"But . . ."

"Now."

He followed her silently out of the restaurant and then to the parking lot. She didn't say a word until she got into her car. Then she started the motor and turned to him. Her face was white and tense.

"Why don't you let it alone?" she said.

"I can't. It's my life, I tell you."

She nodded her head grimly, her hazel eyes flashing. "It sure is. You're going to end up like Nancy Starrett and the rest if you don't watch out. Can't you see that?"

He put his hand desperately on hers.

"I don't care how I end up."

"You'll follow Alicia, I tell you."

"Then I'll follow her," he said despairingly.

"Do you know what you're saying?"

"Yes."

"You're talking like a fool, Kerry."

"Then I'm talking like a fool."

She turned away from him.

"Becky."

She didn't speak.

"Becky, I've got to know. You haven't answered the question. You haven't."

"I know I haven't," she said turning to him.

"Please, Becky."

She looked at him a long time and then she spoke.

"The answer is yes. Is that what you wanted to hear?"

"No, Becky," he said in a very low voice.

Her eyes softened and then she spoke again. "She tried them."

"How did you know?"

"Because we did it together. That's how I know."

"Oh," he murmured.

"And then I gave it up."

"And Alicia?"

She shook her head. "She said she did. But one never knew with Alicia. Isn't that so?"

He kept looking at her.

She reached out and touched his hair tenderly.

And he thought of Alicia doing the same to him.

So many times.

"Kerry, turn away from her. She's gone. Never to come back. Never."

"I know that," he whispered.

"It was her decision to take her life. Alicia always did what she wanted to do. You know that."

He was silent.

"It was, Kerry."

"I don't know," he whispered.

"What do you mean?"

He shrugged silently.

"Kerry, she killed herself. No one else did."

"I don't know," he said.

"Who would want to kill her? Why?"

He looked at her bewilderedly and didn't answer.

He didn't know where the idea had come from.

And it confused and terrified him.

He heard her voice again. "Kerry, you're getting close to the deep end."

"Maybe I am."

"Watch yourself. Please."

"I get thoughts, Becky. I get thoughts. And they don't let me sleep."

"Then you should get help."

He nodded. "Maybe I should."

She looked at him and a sad, poignant look came into her eyes.

"But you won't. You'll just go along as you've been going."

He didn't speak.

"Let's talk again," Becky said.

"All right."

"Call me," she said gently.

Then she drove off, leaving him standing there.

Completely alone.

Chapter

21

I'm over the threshold.
   I know that now.
   Becky is right.
   I'm walking down the corridor.
   Slowly but surely.
   Step by step.
   Following Alicia.
   I can see her beckoning to me.
   In the night I can see her.
   And I follow.
   Because there's nothing I can do about it.
   Nothing.

Chapter

22

The phone rang and he picked it up.

"Kerry?"

It was his father.

"Yes?"

"Well?" There was anger in the voice.

"I haven't made up my mind yet," Kerry said.

"There's nothing to make up. I said I wanted you out here," his father said.

"I know."

"I don't want you in that house alone anymore."

"You've left me alone before," Kerry said and his voice was hard.

"I know I have."

"So what's different now?"

There was a slight pause.

"Well?"

"I just don't like it. That's all."

"I'm all right. Stop worrying."

"Kerry."

"Well?"

"I am worried. And you know why?"

"All right. So I know why. So what?"

"Kerry." Again the pause. And then he heard, "Kerry, she was very close to you."

"She was," Kerry said grimly.

"And I can imagine how hard it must have hit you."

"It hit me."

"Then you know how I feel," his father said.

"I know."

"Then come out here."

"I told you I'm thinking it over."

"No."

"Yes."

His father's voice rose. "Do you want me to come back? To cut short my vacation? Is that what you want? Then I'll do it."

"No."

"You're going to force me to."

There was a silence.

Kerry looked around him at the walls and then out to the gray, sullen sky.

"All right," he said. "I'll come out."

"Good. That's good to hear. Very good."

"But only for a while."

"Sure. Just come out here."

"I'll take the first plane I can get. Okay?"

"Good enough, Son."

"Anything else?"

"Lucy sends her love."

And he wanted to say, Who is Lucy?

"Tell her I send her mine."

"Thanks, Son. I will."

"Goodbye, Dad."

"Goodbye, Kerry."

Then he heard the click.

And for some reason there were tears in his eyes.

Chapter

23

Becky Cobb drove him to the airport. He felt good sitting beside her, looking out at the morning sky.

For the first time in days he felt calm and at peace with himself.

"I'm glad that you're going, Kerry," she said glancing at him.

He nodded. "It'll be nice to get away for a while."

"That's it."

I'll start to breathe again, he thought.

"You'll be just fine, Kerry."

He smiled at her. "Think so?"

"I know so."

"It's what you wanted me to do."

"Right."

They drove along the sunlit highway and everything was warm and pleasant around them.

"I'll see you when I get back, Becky?"

"If you want to."

"I do," he murmured.

She smiled at him. "Then we'll see each other."

He looked away from her and into the sparkling sky. And then he leaned back in his seat and softly closed his eyes.

The wind rippled gently through his hair.

And it was then that he felt Alicia's long tapering fingers touching the strands.

Tenderly.

And it was then that he heard Alicia's ghostly, melodic laughter.

Hovering about him.

He quickly, fearfully, opened his eyes.

The soft laughter faded back and away.

"Becky," he said.

"Yes?"

"Nothing," he said.

"What?"

He shrugged and was silent.

The wind rippled gently through his hair.

Chapter

24

And yet for two full weeks he did forget Alicia. His father and Lucy went out of their way to make him feel happy.

To smile and even to laugh.

He let them do it.

For the first time in years he felt himself draw close to his father. As if he never knew the man intimately and now suddenly, subtly, he started to see bright facets that were hidden away from him.

He started to understand the man.

And to forgive him.

They were sitting at an outdoor café on one of the side streets of Spoleto. Lucy had gone off to do some shopping and now the two were alone. It was close to evening and the shadows were beginning to come in. The long shadows.

His father was drinking a martini and he was holding a half-filled glass of beer. They had been talking, just pleasant, desultory talk, and now a silence fell over them, a meditative silence.

Far in the distance, a church bell sounded, faint and thin;

he listened to it, a glow in his eyes, until the sound was gone.

Kerry sat there, looking lazily about him, at the people at the other tables, at the cobbled street that sloped up and away till it ended at a dusty stone wall . . . and then he turned slowly back to his father.

His quiet, pensive father.

He began to study his father's profile.

The clean lines of it.

You're a very handsome man, he said to himself.

It's easy to see why women are attracted to you. I can just walk at your side down any street and watch their eyes light up as you pass by.

And you're very aware of it, aren't you?

How could it be otherwise?

You're a selfish man.

You can be hard and aggressive.

That's why you've gotten to the top.

Now you call your shots.

A lot of people in your game fear you.

And yet you can be very good and generous.

And you love me very much.

I can see that now.

Over the years I was never sure until now.

It's a good feeling. Such a good feeling.

"Dad," he said gently.

His father slowly turned to him.

"Yes?"

"Mom still loves you."

His father looked silently at him, but his face paled just a bit. "You know that, don't you?"

"Yes, Kerry."

"And you?"

His father finished off his martini and then motioned to the waiter and pointed to his glass.

"You want another beer, Kerry?"

Kerry shook his head. "No. Thanks."

"All set?"

Kerry nodded. "Yes."

He watched the man's finger play with the rim of the glass.

"Maybe I shouldn't have brought it up, Dad."

His father shook his head. "You have every right to, Kerry. She's your mother and I'm your father."

He waited until the waiter set down his martini and went off and then he spoke again. "You remember the time I wanted you to follow me? To become a champion swimmer. And you easily could have become one."

Kerry didn't answer.

"You didn't do it because you hated me then. Isn't that so?"

Kerry still didn't speak.

"You took the easy out. You said you just didn't like competition. But that wasn't the truth. Was it?"

"It wasn't," Kerry said.

His father smiled sadly. "But if I asked you today?"

"I think I would do what you wanted."

They were silent.

"Kerry?"

"Yes?"

"I still love your mother."

"And?"

"And we couldn't live together. You know that. You saw how bitter our quarrels were. You suffered through all that."

"I did," Kerry said in a low voice.

His father leaned forward and gripped his hand. "Kerry, listen to me. Love doesn't do it all. There's something else needed. And I just don't know what it is."

And Kerry thought, I could've been happy with Alicia. And she with me.

I know that.

God, how I know that.

And she knew it, too.

She did.

Then why did she kill herself?

Why?

No.

She couldn't have.

She couldn't have done it, knowing the pain it would bring me.

Knowing that finally she was killing me, too.

He heard his father's voice.

"I find life much easier with Lucy."

"I can see that."

His father smiled. "You do?"

"Yes."

"I like to hear you say that, Kerry."

His father patted his hand.

They were silent again.

"Do you love her?" Kerry asked softly.

His father shook his head.

"No."

"Oh," Kerry murmured.

And he felt sorry for Lucy.

"She knows that. And she's willing to go along with it," his father said.

"Is she?"

"Yes."

For how long? Kerry thought.

I can see you getting yourself another wife.

In due time.

What will her name be?

Eleanor? Joan? Mary?

What, Dad?

His father looked sharply at him and then spoke. "Kerry listen to me."

"Yes?"

"You're young. And the young always want answers. Instant answers."

"So?"

"So there are no absolute answers in this life. None. You live and that's all there is to it." A poignant, almost desperate look had come into the man's eyes. "This is a tough, tough world. A heartless one. One that tries to beat you down every minute of the day. You do your best to survive. To keep your sanity. And a bit of your integrity. Just a bit. And that's enough. And if you do that then you're way ahead of the game."

They were silent.

The people at the next table got up and left and Kerry watched them saunter out onto the cobbled street.

Their shadows moved slowly along the old, glistening stones.

Blocks of stone that lay there through the long, dark centuries.

People had been killed on these streets, he thought.

Stabbed to death in medieval and Renaissance times.

Their glistening blood ran over those uncaring stones.

No one cared then.

No one cares now.

The rains wash the blood away.

He turned back to his father. "What you're saying is that one has to make adjustments. No matter what happens to him. Isn't that it?"

"Yes."

"And I should forget Alicia. Turn away from her. As if she never lived or died."

His father shook his head. "No. I'm not asking you to do that."

"Everybody is," Kerry said. "All my friends."

"They're wrong."

"What do you mean?"

His father sighed. "Believe me. You'll never forget her. The same as I will never forget your mother. She's with me every day. Every day, Kerry."

Kerry looked silently at him.

"But you'll learn to go on living without her. Because life says you have to. And there's no other way. The same as I've learned to go on living without your mother. Do you understand?"

Kerry didn't answer.

"Do you?"

"I guess I do," Kerry said finally.

"You mean that?"

"Yes."

His father smiled sadly at him, finished his drink and then rose. "Let's go find Lucy," he said.

"All right."

"Come along, Son." He said the last word softly.

When they got out onto the cobbled street, he put his arm about Kerry.

"I'm glad you came over, Kerry."

"I am, too, Dad."

"I never asked you. How was the plane trip?"

"Fine. No problems."

"How did you like first class?"

Kerry shook his head.

"I didn't go that way."

"Why not?"

"I changed the ticket for coach."

His father stopped. "Why?"

"Well, I just didn't want to spend the money."

"But I have a lot of money."

"Seemed to be throwing it away. I was comfortable in coach."

"You're just like your mother."

"I guess so."

They walked along and didn't speak for a while.

Two tall, well-set, handsome figures.

"You had me very frightened," his father said, suddenly and quietly.

That I was going to follow Alicia and the others?

Is that it, Dad?

"I didn't sleep much, Kerry."

Frightened that I was going to kill myself?

"I'm sorry, Dad," he said.

His father smiled at him. "But I feel much better now," he said. "Much better."

The shadows became darker as he spoke.

"I do, too," Kerry said.

They walked on into a starless night.

Chapter

25

It was toward the very end of the performance of *Pagliacci*, just as Canio was about to plunge the knife into Nedda's heart, that Kerry felt himself tremble and go cold all over.

The image of Alicia came to him.

Alicia lying on the seat of the silver-gray car.

Her face white and dead.

Canio raised his hand and Kerry almost rose from his seat and was about to shout:

Don't. Don't do it.

He put his fist to his mouth to keep the words from tumbling out.

You mustn't kill another human being. Especially one that you have loved so much.

You mustn't.

But then Canio did plunge the knife.

Nedda lay dead.

Alicia at her side.

And at the end Canio turned to the audience and spoke the heartbreaking words:

La commedia é finita.

The comedy is ended.

Kerry sat silently while his father and Lucy applauded the actors as they came out for their curtain calls.

He knew then that he had to go back home.

Back to Alicia.

And when they came out under a starlit sky and strolled over to an outdoor café, he turned to his father.

"Dad."

"Yes?"

"I think I'll be going back home."

"What?"

"I'd very much like to."

"Why?"

"It's time."

His father shook his head. "No, Kerry."

"But, Dad . . ."

"You'll come along with us to Florence. We're set there for two weeks."

"I'd rather not."

His father looked at him and was silent.

"We have rented a villa in the hills," Lucy said. "You'll have a great time with us. You're having one now, aren't you?"

"Yes," Kerry said. "I am."

"So come along."

"Just can't, Lucy."

"Why?"

"I feel like a fifth wheel," Kerry said.

"You're not. Not at all. We want you with us," she said.

They went into the café and picked out a table and sat down.

"It's lovely in the hills," Lucy said. "That's what everybody says."

"I know," Kerry said. "I've been there."

"Change your mind."

107

"I'd like to, Lucy. But I can't."

"For me?"

He smiled at her but didn't speak.

Kerry waited until his father ordered and then he turned to him.

"Dad, I have a lot of things to take care of."

"For example?"

"College stuff. I've neglected it."

His father glanced at Lucy and then back to Kerry. "You just want to get home. Is that it?"

"Yes."

"I don't know, Kerry."

"Dad, I'm okay now."

"You sure?"

"Believe me. I'm okay."

His father looked searchingly at him. "I guess there's no changing your mind," he finally said.

"There isn't."

"Even if I begged you?" Lucy said gently.

"I'm afraid so, Lucy."

The waiter brought the drinks and then went away.

"Well?" Kerry asked.

His father drank and then slowly put down his glass.

"All right, Kerry. You want to go, then go."

"Thanks, Dad."

"But take first class this time."

"Whatever you say."

"Stop being like your mother. Don't save me money."

And then he laughed.

But his eyes never left Kerry's face.

He's still worried about me, Kerry thought.

And frightened.

I am, too.

Yet I must go.

Alicia is pulling me back to her.

Chapter

26

All the way over on the night flight he kept looking out of the window and thinking of the plunging knife.

Hearing again the piercing scream of Nedda.

And then seeing Alicia falling, falling to lie still.

So very still.

He kept seeing her and then a thought, like a lightning flash, burst upon him and left him shivering.

Someone has killed Alicia, he said to himself.

Someone has done it to her.

She could not have killed herself.

Not Alicia.

From the first time Marian Kent called me, I've felt that.

Not Alicia.

Deep down.

When she said, Alicia has killed herself, I didn't believe it.

Deep down.

I didn't.

I know it now.

I know it.

But do I?

Do I?

This is madness.

Sheer madness.

I can't go on much longer this way.

I can't.

I'm walking down the dark corridor and I must turn around and go back.

I must.

Or this will kill me.

It will.

He turned away from the terrifying night sky and leaned back in his seat and closed his anguished, weary eyes, closed them shut. He fell into an instant sleep.

Kerry?

Yes, Alicia?

It's over with. Can't you see that?

I can't, Alicia.

Let me rest.

No.

Let me, Kerry.

But I can't.

You have to. I must rest and you must rest. You must. Or you will soon follow me, my love. Into death.

I just can't stop.

Why not?

Because I must find out the truth.

Truth?

Yes.

And then he heard her soft, ghostly laughter.

Alicia, stop it.

And then her voice.

Mocking and harsh.

Who in this life ever learns the truth?

Who, Kerry?

"Kerry?"

He slowly opened his eyes and he saw the stewardess leaning over him.

"Yes?"

"Kerry," she said again softly.

He stared up at her concerned face.

"I've brought you a blanket," she said.

"What?"

"You were shivering from the cold."

"Oh."

She deftly tucked the blanket about him.

"There. Doesn't that feel better?"

"Yes."

"Do you want some hot coffee?"

"No. Thanks."

He watched her go off and then he turned to the window and looked out at the dark, impenetrable night.

Chapter
27

He was at the airport waiting for his luggage when he became aware of a man standing close to him, a short stocky man with a hard face.

Kerry's bag finally came down the carousel and he reached over to get it, but the man was quicker and he picked up the bag in one of his big hands.

"I'm sorry," Kerry said. "but that's mine."

The man smiled grimly. "I know it is."

Kerry didn't speak.

"You're Kerry Lanson, aren't you?"

"Yes."

"Then I have the right bag."

"What do you mean?"

"Mr. Kent sent me to greet you."

Kerry stared at him.

"He's concerned about you." The man spoke in a quiet even voice that contrasted strongly with his harsh, rugged face. His eyes were blue and cold.

"Peter Kent knows every move you make. I'm here to welcome you back from Spoleto."

He turned and started walking out to the parking lot, still holding the bag.

Kerry turned and silently followed him.

The man paused. "Your girlfriend is out there waiting for you."

"I know," Kerry said.

"Becky Cobb. Isn't that her name?"

Kerry didn't answer.

"Beautiful. Like Alicia Kent. But in her own way, eh Kerry? You know how to pick them, don't you? Rich and beautiful."

Kerry still was silent.

The man laughed harshly. "I told you, Peter Kent knows every move you make. And when he's ready he will make his." He set the bag down on the pavement. His cold blue eyes were set upon Kerry.

"You're pretty fast with the girls, aren't you? You get rid of one and now you have another. Handsome is as handsome does, eh, kid?"

Then he said in a grim voice. "Good to have you home, murderer."

The man turned and walked away.

Chapter

28

They rode along the sunlit highway, he sitting quietly at Becky's side. He glanced at her brown hair flowing in the soft wind and then turned back to the road, a hopeless look in his eyes, his face tight and sad.

"Kerry?"

"Yes?"

"You were quiet when I drove you to the airport. And now you're just as quiet when I drive you away from it."

"Am I?"

"Yes."

He shrugged and smiled at her.

She patted his knee. "That's a little better."

"I'm sorry, Becky."

"That's all right."

She stopped at a red light and turned to him, her hazel eyes smiling but deep in them a searching look. "You have a good time?"

He nodded. "I did, Becky. They went out of their way for me."

"How'd you like your new mother?"

"Lucy?"

"Uh-huh."

"Liked her very much. She was good company."

"Think the marriage will last?"

"Last?"

"Say, ten years? That's a lifetime in our set."

"Oh."

"Five?"

The light changed and she drove on.

"It'll be gone in about three years," Kerry said.

"Why? Because of Lucy or your father?"

"My father."

"He's too handsome for his own good," Becky said.

"No. It's not that at all."

"Then what is it?"

He hesitated before he spoke again. "There's a cruel and selfish streak in him. A streak that he can't handle. I guess that's it."

She glanced over to him. "We all can be selfish and cruel, Kerry," she said gently.

He shook his head. "I know that. He's a good man and I love him. But he can't handle that streak. Just can't do it."

The same as I can't handle what's happening to me now, he thought.

That's how life is.

And what can you do about it?

Nothing.

You're caught and there's nothing you can do.

"Alicia could be selfish and cruel. Marian Kent feared her," she said.

He looked sharply over to Becky. "I thought they got along very well."

"They did. And they didn't."

"Alicia once told me that she loved Marian more than her

own mother. And I believed her." He spoke low, as if to himself.

"And she believed it when she said that," Becky said quietly.

"But it wasn't so?"

"With Alicia how was one to know?"

How?

And he thought of the time he had called her a sphinx.

She had laughed.

But her eyes were dark when she laughed.

"Yes," he murmured. "How was one to know?"

"Let's leave it alone," Becky said. "I shouldn't have opened it up."

They didn't speak again until she left him off at the house.

"Thanks for driving me," he said. "I appreciate it, Becky."

"No sweat."

He picked up the bag and turned to the black and empty house.

"Kerry?"

"Yes?"

"Want to see me Saturday night?" she asked gently. "If you're not doing anything."

I'm not, he thought.

I'm all alone again.

Alone and frightened.

Why did I come back?

"Well, Kerry?"

He could see the concern on her face.

"All right," he said.

"How's seven?"

He nodded silently.

"I'll pick you up then," she smiled.

And then he stood there watching her drive off.

Feeling Alicia at his side.

Chapter

29

He was sitting looking at the dark, shimmering waters of his pool when Laurie Kent came out of the night and stopped at the edge of the patio and stood there hesitantly.

He got up.

"Laurie?"

She went slowly to one of the chairs and sat down.

"Kerry," she said.

"Yes?"

"I shouldn't be here. But I . . . I had to see you."

He didn't speak.

"I've been rotten to you," she said without looking at him.

"What do you mean?"

Then he saw her lips tremble. "I had to come here. I had to."

She spoke in a low voice, so low he could barely hear her words.

He waited for her to speak again.

All about them the night was dark and expectant.

"I missed you while you were away," she said.

"Did you?"

She nodded and now he could see the glisten of tears in her eyes.

"Sometimes I came here and just looked at your house," she said.

The fragrance of her body was in the air about him, soft and penetrating.

"Kerry?"

"Yes?"

"You must despise me for what I did to you."

He looked at her. "Laurie, I don't know what you're talking about."

She shook her head and her blonde hair gleamed softly in the night.

"You do," she said.

He kept looking at her and for some strange, unsettling reason, he found himself thinking of her mother.

Of Marian Kent and her calm blue eyes.

So calm and steady and clear.

Marian Kent on the golf course, during a match, about to try a difficult and crucial putt, her nerves completely under control.

Her jaw set, with a grim determination, the eyes cold and hard.

He heard Laurie's low voice.

"I lied and now my father hates you bitterly. And my mother doesn't even want to hear me say your name."

"Lied about what?"

"The night of Alicia's death."

"What do you mean?" Kerry asked.

"I never even saw Alicia that night. Never."

A great chill went over him.

"What?" he said.

"I wasn't even in the house when she came in."

He came close to her. "Then she never screamed at you? Never ran to her room and slammed the door shut? Never had a wild look in . . ."

He broke off and couldn't speak anymore.

"Never," Laurie murmured.

She looked fearfully up at Kerry.

"It was all a lie, Kerry."

"But why? Why?" His voice cracked and he turned away from her.

"Kerry, I never thought my father would blame you. I didn't, Kerry. You must believe me."

He slowly turned back to her. "Why did you do it, Laurie? Why?"

"I was afraid. Of my mother."

"Marian?"

"Kerry, she can be very hard on me when she's angry and upset. She's as strong as a man. She can hurt. Kerry, you don't know her as I do. You don't."

He stared at her silently.

Who knows anybody anymore? he thought bitterly.

It's all become darkness and chaos.

We're living in a hell.

"Please, Kerry."

She reached out pleadingly and put her hand on his.

It was warm and trembling.

"She wanted me to stay home that night. But I slipped out and came back very late. In the morning I could see that she was angry and suspicious of me."

He drew his hand away from her.

"Kerry, please don't look at me that way. Please," she begged.

"Why did you do it to Alicia? Why?"

Her face suddenly tightened and then he heard her speak

in a low and harsh voice. "Because I hated Alicia. And this was my way of paying her back. Let them all think she was on drugs that night. Let them."

"Paying her back for what, Laurie?"

"She was always cruel to me."

"That's a lie."

"Kerry, you didn't know her."

"I did know her," he shouted and his voice echoed bitterly against the night. "I knew her better than anybody alive or dead."

"You didn't live with her."

"I didn't have to," he said in a breaking voice.

"Kerry."

"Let me alone."

He closed his lips shut and fought back the tears.

She went over to him.

"Kerry, everybody was afraid of her. Even her father. You must believe me."

"No. No."

"She'd take control of our world and nobody would dare stop her. If she told her father to cut us off without a cent, he'd have to do it."

He put his hand up as if shielding his face.

"I don't want to hear any more."

"Alicia could be generous and loving and good. That's the side she showed you. You didn't see the other."

"I saw all of Alicia. All."

Laurie shook her head. "No, Kerry. You didn't. She was a genius. Years ahead of herself. Like a grown and mature woman. Everybody knew that. A genius." Her voice hardened. "But she could be an evil one. I know. I tell you, I know."

"No more," he said. "No more."

He turned away from her and went over to his chair and sat down.

Then he bowed his head and closed his eyes in pain.

She came close to him.

"Kerry, I'm sorry. Terribly sorry."

She waited for him to speak, but he was silent.

"Now you must hate me, too," she said.

"I don't hate you, Laurie," he said in a low and weary voice.

But he didn't look up at her.

"You do."

She didn't speak anymore.

The silence of the night hovered over them.

He could feel the soft fragrance of her body in the air about him.

And he thought of Alicia bending her head to him, her eyes glowing.

The fragrance faded away.

He sat there, head still bowed.

"Laurie," he said gently. "Alicia loved you like a sister. I know that. She had her moods. I know that, too. But she loved you. She did, Laurie."

Then he looked up and saw that she was gone.

Chapter
30

He went into the den and looked through the record collection till he found *Pagliacci*. Then he put on the very last scene and stood listening to it.

Till he heard the last words.

La commedia é finita.

The comedy is over, he said to himself.

Nedda lies dead.

And the comedy is over.

He turned out the lights and went slowly up the stairs and into his room. He lay down on his bed without undressing.

He closed his eyes and tried to sleep.

She is dead.

Let her rest.

Let her sleep.

She lies under the earth now, her eyes closed.

Let her sleep.

Sleep.

Sleep.

Sleep. . . .

Chapter

31

But at three o'clock in the morning he suddenly awoke and sat up staring into the darkness, his face pale, his lips trembling, the palms of his hands hot and moist.

Nedda did not kill herself, he whispered.

No.

Someone killed her.

Someone killed Alicia.

And I know who did it.

I've always known.

Deep, deep within me I've always known.

He opened his lips and cried out:

"Alicia."

His voice shattered the darkness and a fierce light came into his eyes. He reached over to the night table and picked up the phone.

I may be going mad, he said to himself.

But I'm coming closer to the truth.

The blinding truth.

Chapter

32

"Kerry?" Her voice was sleepy and anxious.

"Yes, Mom. Did I wake you?"

"Kerry, it's midnight out here. I've had a hard day. What's wrong?"

I must control myself.

Speak quietly.

"I'm sorry, Mom. I couldn't sleep and I wanted to talk to you."

I did want to speak to her.

To hear her voice.

I feel so alone.

So desperately cold and alone.

"What is it, Kerry?"

"I wanted to ask you a question. About Alicia."

"Alicia?"

"Alicia Kent."

"Kerry, you're sure nothing is wrong? Please tell me."

"Mom, you said they found a trace of a drug in her when . . . when . . ."

He paused and didn't go on.

"Yes, Kerry?"

"Was there anything else?"

"What do you mean?"

"Were there any needle marks?"

"Yes. There were. On her arm."

He held the receiver tight in his hand. "Mom."

"Yes?"

"Is it possible that someone else could have made those marks?"

"What are you driving at?"

"Is it possible?" His voice was hoarse. "From your experience?"

"Yes. It is," she said.

He leaned back against the pillow and didn't speak.

"Kerry?"

Then he heard her say his name again.

"Mom?"

"Yes?"

"I'm okay," he murmured. "Thanks for the information."

"I don't understand."

"Then let it alone. We'll talk of something else."

"But . . ."

"Something else, Mom."

"All right," she sighed.

"How's Maltby?" he asked.

"He's fine. Just saw him a few hours ago."

"You see a lot of him."

"I guess I do, Kerry."

"Do you think you'll ever marry him?"

"Maltby? No. He's just a dear friend and colleague."

"Will you ever marry again?"

"Of course. Why do you ask?"

"Just making conversation. Let's make some more. How's the weather out there?"

"Kerry," she said. "You're acting very strangely."

"Am I?" He laughed.

"It's a strange world, Mom. A very strange one. Or didn't you notice it?"

There was a silence.

"Mom."

"Yes?"

"You didn't tell me how the weather is out there?"

"Rain. Lots of rain."

"We've had sun. Lots of sun."

"Kerry?"

"Yes?"

"Why don't you hop a plane and come out here? I'll send you the ticket express mail."

"I don't like rain."

"Kerry, I'd come to see you but I'm tied up. Really tied up."

You're always tied up, aren't you, Mom?

When are you untied?

When?

"I'll think about it," he said.

"Kerry, I'd like to see you and talk to you."

"You're worried about me, aren't you?"

"Yes. Especially when you call me at this hour and talk so strangely."

He laughed.

"I am, Kerry."

"I know."

"Then come out here."

He laughed again. "Mom, I'm your son. You're a survivor and I'm a survivor. Stop worrying. I'll be all right. Have a good sleep. I'm sorry I woke you."

"Kerry, don't hang up yet."

"Got to. I love you."

"I love you too, Kerry. I'm sending you the ticket."

"Good night or is it good morning?"

"I'll call you tomorrow."

"Tomorrow? Tomorrow is today out here already. We're in two different worlds, Mom."

"Kerry, I . . ."

He laughed and hung up, crushing out her voice.

Then he sat there, cold and tense.

His eyes staring through the darkness at the shattering truth.

Chapter
33

He remembered.

Alicia got out of the car, the motor still running, and then he saw her go to a small panel of the closed garage door and stand there pressing many buttons.

He watched her long, tapering fingers moving so quickly over the rows, ever so quickly.

The massive garage door slowly opened and she came back to the car.

"An alarm system, Alicia?"

She nodded. "Yes. And a very intricate one. Coded."

She drove the car into the garage.

"We use it at night. Only the family knows the code. No one else," she said.

"You wouldn't even tell it to me?"

She smiled gently at him. "It's no use. Mathematical. And you're so bad with mathematics. It took me a while to teach it to Laurie. Marian got it in no time."

Then he remembered his saying: "You rich are always protecting yourselves, aren't you?"

"Everybody does these days," she said.

"But you more than everybody else. Isn't that so?"

She didn't answer until they were back under the night stars again, the garage door shut tight.

"We have to, Kerry. There is always someone out there that doesn't like us very much. And with good reason." Then she laughed her soft melodic laugh.

"It's money, Kerry. Money. People kill each other over money. And I have more than everybody else so it naturally follows that someone will kill me for my money. Isn't that so?"

He didn't answer.

"It doesn't amuse you, Kerry. I can see that."

"No, Alicia. It doesn't."

She smiled. "Out here we all die young, Kerry. It comes with the territory. We've seen our close friends die, haven't we? Or have you forgotten Nancy Starrett?"

"I haven't."

"Or . . . What are the names of the others? I seem to forget."

"Cut it out, Alicia."

"You don't like to hear of death, do you?"

"I said stop it, didn't I?"

"Does it scare you?"

"Alicia, why do you go on with this? Do you get a charge out of it?"

"Why? It's a good question."

They stood there in the night, the shadow of the garage door falling over her, like a veil.

He remembered that.

Her face pale in the darkness.

Then he saw a sad, lost look come into her eyes.

"Am I showing you my ugly side again?" she asked gently.

"Yes."

"I'm sorry, Kerry. I just couldn't help it."

"You could. If you tried."

"I did."

"You didn't, Alicia. You seem to enjoy doing this to me."

"No, Kerry. No."

She reached her hand out to his.

But he didn't take it.

She stood there in the shadow and he turned away and was about to leave her.

But he heard her voice. "Kerry, Kerry, I'm the one who is scared to death. Can't you see that? Can't you?"

She began to cry in a low voice.

As he took her into his arms and comforted her, the shadow fell over both of them.

He remembered that.

Chapter

34

Now it had all fallen into place.

And it was all so clear.

The needle marks.

Do it while Alicia is asleep.

Wait for the effect of the drug on her.

Now lift her up and carry her.

It is a short distance from her room to the garage.

And you are strong enough to do it.

Now open the coded door.

Set her into the car and place the book of poems at her side.

Don't forget that. It's important.

"When I have fears that I may cease to be."

That becomes her suicide note to the world.

Now turn on the motor.

Shut the door.

And then go back to the sleeping, silent house.

Wait for morning.

Call Kerry.

Alicia has killed herself. Killed herself.
Just like the others.
Just like them.
Who would ever suspect?
Who?

Chapter
35

It was all in place.

All.

His lips were pale and bloodless when he picked up the phone.

A hard glow in his eyes.

Someone will kill me for money, Kerry.

Someone did, Alicia.

Someone did.

Chapter

36

He sat waiting by the pool and this time it was Marian Kent who came out of the night and stood at the edge of the patio.

He felt a chill go over him as he looked at the silent, strong figure.

The pool light glinted on her blonde hair. Her calm blue eyes were dark and impassive.

He got up.

"I'm here, Kerry," she said.

"Yes, Marian."

"Make it short. Peter is in the house waiting for me. We're going out for the evening."

"Does he know you're here?"

She shook her head. "No one knows."

He stood looking at her and he wondered how much Laurie really knew.

Or suspected.

One would never find out.

Never.

He heard Marian's cold voice. "You wanted to talk to me about Alicia's death," she said.

"Yes."

"You said you now know that she did not commit suicide."

"I do, Marian."

"Then how did she die?"

"She was murdered."

He watched her and there was not even a flicker in the dark blue eyes.

"By whom?"

"You know that better than anybody else in this world, Marian."

"Do I?"

"Yes."

"Tell me."

"You killed her, Marian."

And he could see her that murderous night, her emotions completely under control, as now, her mind cold and precise.

She had carried it all out just as if she were playing under great pressure the last three holes of a golf match.

Each movement completely thought out.

And executed.

"You executed her, Marian," he said.

Her face was like a mask.

Emotionless.

"And her crime?" she asked.

"You saw that sooner or later Peter Kent was going to turn over everything to Alicia."

"He was."

"And that she'd make sure that you and Laurie were forced out into the cold."

"She would have."

"And with the suicides in our town . . . This was the time to do it."

"Yes, Kerry."

This is all so quiet, he thought.

So deathly quiet.

I should be shouting at her and she should be . . .

He heard her voice again. "How did you find all this out?"

"Just by looking through the other end of the telescope, Marian. Changing my perspective."

"I see."

"Everybody saw the death as a suicide. I did, too. And then I was forced to look on it as a murder."

"And then it all fell into place."

"All."

Her eyes looked calmly and coldly at him. "And what are you going to do now?"

"Nothing," he said.

"Nothing?"

"Who will ever believe me? What proof have I?"

Then he saw her smile grimly.

"Kerry," she said.

"Yes?"

"Live with it. Learn to live with it. As I have."

"Then you did kill her?"

"Good night, Kerry."

She turned and started to walk away from him.

"Marian," he shouted. "Peter Kent wants to talk to you."

She stopped and her face whitened.

Then they saw Peter Kent come out of the night, the hard-faced man at his side.

"It's over, Marian," Kerry said in a harsh voice. "And you've lost."

It was then that she began to scream.

136

Chapter
37

He was sitting on Becky Cobb's boat and they were heading out of the inlet and into the open sea.

The day was calm and bright.

The water smooth and level.

They had been talking quietly to each other and now they had lapsed into a warm silence.

He turned from Becky and looked into the shimmering horizon.

He heard the soft, ghostly laugh of Alicia.

Soft and poignant.

And he knew that he would hear it for the rest of his life.

About the Author

Jay Bennett, a master of suspense, was the first writer to win in two successive years the Mystery Writers of America's prestigious Edgar Allan Poe Award for Best Juvenile Mystery. One of his earlier books, *The Skeleton Man*, was nominated for the 1986 Edgar Allan Poe Award. He is the author of many suspense novels for young adults as well as successful adult novels, stage plays, and television scripts. Mr. Bennett lives in Cherry Hill, New Jersey.